THUNDER STRUCK

MIMI FOSTER

Best wishes,

DEDICATION

This book is dedicated to the greatest accomplishment of my life, my daughters. I like to tell myself that I gave them life, but the truth is – they gave it to me. I love you, Betsy, Susie, Katie, Maggie, and Callie.

ACKNOWLEDGMENTS

There aren't many days that go by when there is not someone who touches me and blesses me on this writing journey. No one is more encouraging than my very own leading man, David, to whom I am exceedingly lucky to be married. Mandy Sellet, you have such a gift for defining what's important and helping me see what to let go of (and yes, there is a preposition at the end of that sentence). Debbie Beck, I'm not sure I could have made it this far without you. Stephanie Kirby, you are a daughter of my heart, and thank you for always listening. Anne Eliot, you've taught me so much about this process and kept me focused on what was important. Mike Beck, your insight and knowledge opened up a new world for me. Amy Cesario, thank you for bringing the sunshine no matter what the weather. Dana Kunec Thomas, have I told you lately how glad I am that you're in my life? Robin Shanley Phillips, what a fun way to reconnect. Nick Hahn, thank you for motivating me with your perceptive outlook. To Priscilla Barsotti, my oldest and dearest friend, thank you. Tiffany Black Overhoser, our escapes to this 'new reality' have been so much fun. And MacKenzie Jordan Madsen Foster, I love you to the moon and back. Virginia Henry, you actually *did* give me life, and I thank you for your continual encouragement. Special thanks to Kim Killion and Jennifer Jakes of The Killion Group, Inc., who are the best of the best.

And to my old and new friends who have shared your hours with Callie and Jack in *Thunder Snow*, and your hearts and your support with me, my deepest and sincerest thanks. I hope you like Jordan and Brandan in this ever-expanding community. (Anne Marie Smith, don't ever stop with your notes. You were my first public words of encouragement, and they meant a lot to me.)

Cover models: Harvey Gaudun-Stables and Ryan Natalino

CHAPTER 1

"So I'll see you for lunch tomorrow?" Andrew took my face in his hands and kissed me on the forehead, nose, lips.

"That works for me. I have a dress fitting and a few errands in the morning, but I can meet you at The James by noon."

"You sure you won't stay the night? I promise I'll make it worth your while."

"Three more weeks, then we have the rest of our lives. I'm enjoying our new playfulness. How are *you* holding up?"

"Come home with me and I'll show you," he said, pulling me tight against him.

"You're incorrigible."

He took my face once more and gave me his special kiss. We had made the decision to not sleep together the last month before the wedding, and our relationship was benefiting from a new degree of flirtatiousness.

What a whirlwind it had been. With the planning and arrangements of our upcoming wedding and honeymoon, and the sale of my New York co-op, I'd taken an extended leave of absence from the law firm. An associate who was out of town for a month let me sublet her apartment. Somewhere in the mix I even inherited a Bed and Breakfast in a tiny town in Colorado. I'd done research on the mountain village where it was located, and hoped to talk Andrew into a side trip after the wedding. It sounded romantic.

The past few years had been twelve-hour days with little down time, so this working vacation was a coveted time to unwind. I turned my case files over to Andrew and could easily fill him in if he had questions. It sometimes surprised me that we'd been able to build a relationship, but our working proximity made it convenient, and he had been persistent.

"Good evening, Jordanna." He answered the phone in his distinctive, clipped voice. "Ready to come back to work?" I loved that my father always called me by my given name.

"Not a chance, but thanks for the offer," I said affectionately. "I'm calling to let you know I've cleared my schedule and turned everything over to Andrew. I brought him up-to-date on my caseload, so if you have questions, you can check with him."

"Are you sure he's up to the task?"

"You're not?" I was slightly surprised at his question.

"Oh, don't get me wrong. He seems competent enough, but he doesn't hold a candle to Jordanna Olivia. I trust your judgment, however, so if he's going to be my son-in-law, I'll commence showing him the inner sanctum of Whitman and Burke."

"Thank you. I appreciate your vote of confidence. He's quite clever at handling my clients in a savvy and capable manner."

"That's never been a question, but I'll start giving him more responsibility. Don't be a stranger. Stop in when you're around. Maybe we can do lunch next week? Call Carol and set something up."

"Of course. Thank you, Father."

The September air was brisk and added a degree of bounce to my step. I had a list of things I wanted to accomplish before I met Andrew for lunch. We were meeting a realtor afterwards to look at a Brooklyn Brownstone we were interested in. Finishing two errands, I was lighthearted with my new-found freedom as I entered the third store. The boutique was elegantly subdued, and had been highly recommended. I was looking for lingerie for our wedding night, and the garden-level provided just the right amount of light and privacy for intimate-apparel shopping.

Coming out of the fitting room, I saw Andrew through the tinted window leaving the building across the street. Surprised and pleased to see him, I started to call out when I remembered my scanty attire. Hurrying to the dressing room, I grabbed my phone and headed back to the window to text him and let him know where I was. He turned just then toward the blonde woman who walked out behind him. Their lips almost touched, and I thought I was mistaken that it was Andrew, so I set my phone down.

He held her face in his hands and kissed her forehead, nose, lips. The breath left my body. His arms embraced the fair-haired beauty who laid her head on his chest as he stroked her in the all-too-familiar way he had done to me so often. I tried to reactivate my brain to grasp what to do next.

Think, Jordan, think. Seconds passed before the adrenaline surged and I became somewhat coherent and focused. I grabbed a robe from a nearby hook and quietly opened the door. Magnifying my phone camera for a close up, I was able to capture several pictures of Andrew holding her face and kissing her before they slowly broke apart. I stepped back and let the door close, imagining that it was closing on a huge part of my life.

Shocked as though I'd been hit by an electric current, I was still able to text to say something had come up and I wouldn't be able to meet, and asked him to cancel our appointment. Watching as he received the message, he immediately ran to catch up with the blonde. He put his arm around her as they walked away.

Was it possible I was mistaken? I looked at the pictures. This was no mistake. I'd been kissed like that too many times to not understand that life as I knew it had been radically altered, and my world was being rocked to its foundation. It was all I could do to hold myself together. The clerk was sweet when I told her something had come up and I'd have to leave without purchasing her diaphanous creations. Alternating between disbelief and anger, I was unsure where to go, what to do. Was there protocol for something like this? The more I wandered, the angrier I got.

I wasn't aware of the miles I walked, but by the time I found myself in front of the advertising agency of my best friend, I was ready to detonate. How do you share this information? When does the trembling stop?

"What is it? What happened?" Jeni said, coming around the desk, taking me by the shoulders.

Too angry to be coherent, I pulled my phone from my purse and showed her the pictures. I saw awareness dawn, and then indignation washed over her. "I was going to make excuses, think maybe you were wrong, maybe it's his cousin, maybe it's not really him, but it's Andrew, isn't it?" she asked with fire in her eyes.

Nodding, I wanted to fling something. It unnerved me that I never saw it coming. I now understood the term 'blindsided.' A thousand questions, and they all came back to, "Was this my fault?"

"Don't you *dare* go there, Jordanna Olivia Whitman! This is *his* fault! You will not share an ounce of guilt, do you hear me?"

"It's not guilt, it's self doubt and anger and disbelief and stupidity in not seeing. What if I had *married* him? And the questions keep coming. How long has it been going on? Who is she? What did he want from me? But I can't seem to get away from, *How could I have been so stupid?*"

"You had no way of knowing. I can be done for the day. Let's get out of here."

As we headed down the elevator, she said, "What are you gonna tell him? Surely you're calling off the wedding?"

"There's no way I can talk to him right now. I'm seeing red. And of *course* I'm calling off the wedding. I'm just not sure where to go now that I sold my co-op. How do you avoid the gigantic spotlight that'll find you when news like this breaks?"

"You can stay at my place. You know me, I'll put a favorable spin to it."

"I wouldn't think of putting you through something like that. God, Jeni, it's gonna be awful."

"Jordan! Remember the letter you got last month about a Bed and Breakfast in some obscure little town? Where was that, Wyoming? Colorado? Did you ever respond?"

"People would think I was running away."

"Who gives a rip? You've got lots of time off. You get to do what you want, especially right now."

"Having a drink sounds like a good option," I suggested hopefully.

"Sounds perfect. Come on."

We drank at several bars, but somewhere along the way I lost count of how many. I *was* aware, however, that with each successive stop, the funny side of today's surprise took hold. We were relaxed and silly by the time we got back to my temporary condo.

"I mean seriously, Jeni, what were the chances I'd be standing right there, right then? Kismet."

The familiar ding of Andrew's text came through. *Sorry you couldn't make it for lunch. I was so lonely without you. Want to meet for drinks?*

Can't make it. Out with Jeni. Will be in touch. Maybe you can find something else fun to do.

Nothing's fun without you.

I couldn't even respond. Good grief, what a snake. How long had he been seeing her? It didn't look as though they'd just met.

"Wanna spend the night with me, Jeni? There's an extra room. My clothes fit you. In the morning we're either on the same page, or you'll talk me down from the cliff. Please?"

"We're diabolical plotters. Of course I will," she said, as we broke into laughter again.

"And you know what else?" I asked after a few minutes of silence. "I was excited about owning a Brownstone."

"Isn't *that* the truth? You might still want to, you just have to wait 'til the dust settles from *this* fallout before you think about taking a major step like that."

Lying on the couch a while later, she asked, "How do you feel? I'm ready to tear him limb from limb. What are *you* thinking?"

"Not a clue. The idea of going to Nederland has some appeal."

"Okay, but we don't decide anything 'til morning," Jeni said. "It's been a long day and your world derailed. We're not necessarily coherent, so let's see how you feel after a good night's sleep."

The morning dawned clear. Surprisingly, so did my brain. With Jeni's encouragement, I was warming to the idea of leaving town. "Not sure where the letter ended up in the confusion of my move, but I remember the name of the realtor that the lawyer mentioned I should contact in case I wanted to sell the place. I'll call her and get whatever details I need. In the meantime, we have to notify the guests, figure out what to do with the gifts, the caterers, the travel arrangements, hotels, the plans."

I'd never considered myself vindictive, but I was ready to proceed. Jeni and I spent the day contacting caterers and venues and making the necessary arrangements to cancel a wedding that had been in the planning stages for months. Then we went to a print shop and waited while we had 'unvitations' printed, as Jeni was calling them. My marketing pal had done a great job designing them.

It was Saturday evening. I had a plane ticket to Denver for Monday noon. I made contact so I knew how to meet Callie Weston when I got there. I hadn't spoken with Andrew since the events of yesterday morning. What surprised me was I didn't feel sad about it; I was angry and embarrassed, but I didn't feel a loss yet. Time away would help me gain perspective. There was no part of me that felt a need to answer his calls. I returned his texts to tell him I was spending the weekend with Jeni attending to wedding matters and would contact him Monday, all of which was true. It's not like he was pining for me.

"I think it's poetic justice," Jeni said, "but I don't have as much at stake as you do. Sure you wanna go through with this?"

"Telling my father will be the worst, but I'm sure he'll find a way to put the famous Wiley Riley twist on it. We both know how adept he is at that sort of thing."

"No question, he's the master. Okay, sweetheart, let's get these addressed."

Everything was in place by early Monday. Arrangements had been canceled, all of the unvites were ready for Jeni to drop in the mail. She was a trooper, staying with me the whole time, talking me through the ups and downs, helping me get the details done. Most important had been her encouragement that life was going to look different soon. I had one last stop to make before my flight.

Knowing he was at work, I used my key to let myself into Andrew's apartment. My purpose was twofold: to make sure I had all of my belongings from his place, and to leave him a copy of the unvite so he'd have some clue what was about to hit him.

Jeni and I discussed the pros and cons of giving him a warning, but it was all the more appealing to think he would know beforehand and there wouldn't be a thing he could do to stop it. I had momentary twinges of doubt about whether or not to go through with it until I saw two wine glasses in the sink, one with a lipstick imprint. I had made the right decision. Much harder would be the phone call to my father during the cab ride.

As Jordan was landing at Denver International Airport, Andrew was arriving home after a tiring day. They hadn't spoken in a while, but he recognized her handwriting on the distinctive envelope on the counter. He immediately looked around hoping nothing was out of place, and made a mental note to remember to be more careful in the future.

It was strange that her key was on the counter. "Jordan?" he called out. "You here?" He let out a sigh of relief as he reassured himself everything appeared to be in order – until he picked up the letter and noticed it was propped against two wine glasses, one with the betrayal of red lipstick on its rim. Tearing open the envelope, he saw the bold, perfect lettering that proclaimed: ***LOVE IS BLIND***. He fell into a chair as he opened the card to see an intimate picture of him kissing Mary Ann with large letters announcing: ***FORTUNATELY, I'M NOT***.

CHAPTER 2

Driving into the charming town nestled in a high mountain valley, I was breathless at the splendor of this enchanting village that overlooks the water. I'd never seen anything to equal the perfection of its location, and there were million dollar homes built next to ramshackle log cabins. The leaves were still on the trees, with just a hint of the coming colors of autumn.

Finally finding my inheritance on the side of a hill, I wondered at this humorous twist of fate. I parked the rental car next to several others in the driveway. The three-story, gun-metal-gray mansion with a turret was like something out of a horror movie. I expected bats and windows covered with webs. The front door creaked on its hinges as I entered. I wouldn't have been surprised to have been greeted by Vincent Price.

"Hello?" I called into cavernous surroundings, listening as my voice echoed against empty walls.

"We're upstairs!" came a lady's voice.

A tall, attractive redhead appeared at the top of the stairs flanked by three men.

"Hi! You must be Jordan! We've been expecting you! Did you have any trouble finding it? Welcome to Colorado!"

"Thank you," I said, looking around the empty room. "Not much trouble. Your directions were excellent."

"Good, I'm glad." She came down the large stairway that fanned out as it flowed into the main level. Two of the men went back into an upstairs room while the tallest followed her.

Extending her hand, she said, "So nice to meet you. I'm Callie Weston. This is my husband Jack. We were trying to get things done before you got here, but it's gonna take a few more days to get you up and running."

"Only a few?" I said, smiling as I looked around.

Callie laughed. "Well, the basics, at least. We got the plumbing working, but the house has been vacant so long, it'll be a few days before they have the electrical up to code."

"Wow, thank you! I hadn't given much thought to what was on the other side of the letter. It didn't occur to me it wouldn't be habitable."

"It'll be fine soon. Jack and his men got a bed over here, but we'd love for you to stay at our cabin until things are ready. It's vacant, and you'd want for nothing."

"Your generosity is overwhelming, but I'd prefer not to get settled somewhere else then try to acclimate here. I don't want to cause trouble, but is it all right if I stay here?"

Callie and Jack looked at each other. "You don't look like you're used to roughing it," he said. "There won't be electricity for a few days, but there is running water. Of course, without electricity there won't be any *hot* water, but it's up to you."

Trying not to be discouraged, I said, "I'd like to stay if I could."

"Then we'll make it happen," Callie said encouragingly. Jack headed back upstairs.

"Jack'll make sure it's as usable as possible. Do you have luggage? I'll help you."

Heading out the front door, I called over my shoulder, "Of course you won't help me, but thanks for the offer."

"I'm pregnant, not an invalid."

"I bet Jack wouldn't agree. There's not much. It won't take long."

Callie showed me to a large room upstairs to the right of the staircase. Wallpaper was missing in places, but the antique chandelier was a work of art. "This is a dichotomy." I laughed. "1890s cut-crystal and brass light fixture with 1980s blue floral wallpaper. Quite the contrast."

"I know this has to be different than what you're used to, but this place has such wonderful bones."

"Excuse me?" I said, imagining skeletons in closets.

With apparent humor, she said, "Sorry, in my world I try to help people understand the difference between the skin and bones of a house. The bones are the structure, the foundation, the location, the soundness of the building itself, the things that can't be changed. The skin is easy to change—paint and wallpaper, light fixtures, countertops, floors. This place has great bones, but its skin needs some work."

From that perspective, I was able to look through the outdated colors and decorating. There was a four poster bed, a dresser, two end tables, two lamps. "You did all of this?" I asked, surprised.

"I had them finish what needed to be done in here before they did anything else. There's a bathroom attached, so no matter what else is going on, except for the painting and whatever else you want to do in here, this room is done and they can work around you. You'll have a modicum of privacy in the confusion."

"That was awfully nice of you to do for an outsider."

"The house has been in your family since it was built. That practically makes you a native. Besides, I'm tickled to have a female my age moving here. Being surrounded by a bunch of good looking men can get tiring after a while," she said, smiling. "And this place needs someone to love it. I'm glad you decided to come out."

"I've only committed for the next month or so. I've got a busy law practice in New York so I'm just here for a break. I need to figure out what to do with this place, then take some time to figure out what to do with my life. Hard to do when you're working a seventy-hour week in the craziness called Manhattan."

"Then you've come to the right place. Lots of people run away here. Never know what you're gonna find."

"When are you due?"

"A little less than two months. On one hand I'm ready, on the other I keep thinking of what needs to be done first, but she'll get here when it's time."

"A little girl, that's exciting."

"Charlotte Rose. She'll be spoiled rotten," she said. "She'll be the apple of her daddy's eye, and Jack's been around town for a long time so everyone's thinking of her as their own."

"You're so blessed—like an extended family."

"Very extended. And just so you have a sense of who's running around your house—Jack runs a building enterprise. When we heard you were coming, he got his best guys to get as much done as possible. Brandan is Jack's foreman for the Denver area, Miles is the foreman for areas outside of Denver."

"I can't believe you did this for me."

"We did it for you *and* we did it for the town. Everyone's pleased the place has a new owner. It's been lonely on this hill for too long and it needs new life. The grounds are overgrown, there's a lot of work to do, but it'll be worth it if someone's willing to take the time to love it."

"I'm not sure I'm your answer, Callie, but if I'm not, we'll make sure *someone* is before I go back."

"We'll see."

CHAPTER 3

Before it was dark, Callie and I headed to the local store to purchase flashlights, oil lamps, and battery powered lamps. The sun was setting as we got back. I hadn't grasped what happens in an unfamiliar house when the sun goes down and there's no electricity. It would be fun and scary at the same time. It had been a long weekend and I was beyond exhausted.

Jack came down with the others and introduced us, and I understood what Callie meant about being surrounded by good looking men. The lanterns cast an eerie glow as we exchanged pleasantries. Callie again offered to let me stay at their cabin, but I didn't want to be spoiled with luxuries if this was going to be my home for a while.

I was looking forward to peace and quiet, something I hadn't known in years. Tired as I climbed the stairs, I still had a keen sense of anticipation. I refused to think about Andrew. It wasn't time yet, and it was easy to ignore that situation in this place far removed from the familiar. There would be plenty of time, but not tonight. As I drifted off to sleep, I tried to remember when the last time was I heard the chirping of crickets.

Loud noises woke me, and it took a few seconds to get my bearings. The shower water was as cold as anything coming from a refrigerator door, certainly enough to wake me up. I slipped into warm clothes and went to find the source of the noise.

"Good morning?" I said to the man with short, dark hair standing on the ladder.

"Hey, Jordan. Sorry if the hammering woke you up. We want to get your electricity on as soon as possible."

"Please, forgive me. I was tired and it was dark and I'm afraid I don't remember your name."

"I'm Miles, that's Brandan," he said, pointing behind me.

I turned to say hello, and knew I must have been distracted last night to not have remembered this man's face, the wave of his hair, his piercing eyes. "I know we met, but I'm surprised how different things look in the light of day." I was proud of myself that my accelerated heart rate wasn't evident in my voice. He was all-kinds-of handsome.

"That's true with most of life, isn't it?" he said.

"You look familiar. Could we possibly have met before last night?" Miles and Brandan exchanged a look.

"I assure you I'd remember, but it's not likely," he said.

"I'm sorry I don't have any coffee or food to offer. Is there anywhere nearby I can grab some?"

"Don't worry about us," said Miles, hammering again. "We bring whatever we need for the day."

"It's gonna be a long day or two," Brandan said. "It's your house, so feel free to come and go as you please. We'll have it functional as soon as we can. Callie left some fruit in the kitchen if you want something to eat."

"How nice of her. I'll grab something while I explore. I've been in old houses before, but nothing like this."

"Ask if you have questions. This one has a lot of character, a lot of history."

I started in the basement. Some might have found it disturbing with no light, stone walls, cobwebs, but I was fascinated. It looked invitingly eerie. One of my first jobs would be to get the covers off the windows and get light in here. I was already making plans.

On the main floor, I stopped in the parlor and was sidetracked by what appeared to be hair in the plaster that had been dislodged onto the floor. "Gross, is that hair?"

"Yeah," Brandan said. "Inside the walls are wood slats called lath. When they mixed horse hair with the wet plaster, it reinforced the plaster so it didn't fall off when they pushed it through the lath. For being over a hundred and twenty years old, this house is as sturdy as it was the day she was built."

Picking up a piece and examining it, I knew I had a lot to learn. This was a new experience, and something pulled at my soul to know more. "Whenever you think of things like this and want to tell me, I'm all ears. It's intriguing, and I want to know everything I can about the house. Don't ever think you'll be boring me if you want to share."

Miles nodded toward Brandan and said, "He's the history buff. Anything you want to know, ask him. He's like a walking encyclopedia."

When I looked at Brandan, I was surprised at the skip of my pulse. A rebound relationship was the last thing I needed. I might be a mess of emotion, but as long as I was aware, I'd be fine.

"I'm gonna check out the turret, so I'll see you guys in a while."

"No one's been up there in a long time. Might find lots of spider webs, so be prepared," Miles said.

"Thanks for the warning!" I noticed one piece of furniture as I hurried through the main floor. A paint-stained tarp layered in years of dust and drywall powder covered a magnificent piano. I didn't play, but knew when I touched a few of the keys that it was dreadfully out of tune. How had it survived all these years without being ruined?

"We didn't know whether you'd want to keep that here or not, but it's a beaut," Brandan said from the doorway. "There's a piano tuner in Boulder who can make it good as new if you don't want to get rid of it."

I was displeased with what he was doing to my heart rate. "I love it being here, quite a conversation piece. You're welcome to move it to the center of the room to work around it, but absolutely, let's get it restored. One of my fondest memories was sitting with my grandfather while my grandmother played. I'm thrilled it's here. Thank you."

The staircase was wide and curved at the bottom and the top. It led to a hallway on either side, both of which had smaller stairways that led to the third floor. I headed toward the right side to the south of the building, looking for the turret.

'Enchanting' was the word for the dusty, webby, circular enclosure. I held my breath for a moment to contain my delight. The water glistened in the distance through the cloudy window. This was where I wanted my bedroom. There were wide oak planks on the floor, an empty bookshelf to the left, and a tall, antique armoire that was securely locked to the right of the window. Curious, I pulled my trusty knife from my back pocket to see if it might slip into the lock opening, but it was too wide. The house felt alive, even after its years of neglect, and I was fanciful in thinking of all the secrets it must hold. I didn't want to acknowledge that it felt like home, but under different circumstances I could see myself living here.

There appeared to be no direct passage to the other side of the third floor, so I took the other set of stairs from the north side. This room had sharply gabled ceilings and a small window that had a slight view of the Reservoir. I'd want to put a doorway through to the other side and make this my office. I was enamored.

Miles and Brandan were working in the dining room. "I have a question. There's so much to be done, not just getting rid of wallpaper and teal carpeting, but I'd like each room on the second floor to have a bath, add a laundry, have work done on the third floor, a new kitchen, obviously paint the whole thing, it appears to need a new roof, and I'm sure the list will go on. I know you're getting the electrical done as a favor to Callie, but can I hire you to help with the renovation?"

Miles told me he'd taken time off because his mother had been sick. She passed away recently and he was just returning to work. He'd be able to help some, but had to get back in the loop for Jack. Brandan remained silent for a bit. "We can find the crew for what you need. What time frame are you thinking?"

"Is two months reasonable?"

"With the right people, sure. Think about what you want while we finish the electrical. Take a few days, get a feel for the place. We have the resources."

"I'm in a run-down Victorian in the middle of nowhere, and I feel like a kid in a candy store."

"Have you seen the cottage yet?" Brandan asked. "Talk about work that needs to be done."

"*No*! I didn't even know there *was* a cottage! I'll see you in a while!" I rushed to the back door when Brandan stopped me.

"Wait! Don't go getting ahead of yourself. Just hold on." He opened a drawer in the kitchen and took out a key ring with lots of keys. "It's bolted so squatters don't get in, and the windows are boarded up, so I'll come with you." He picked up a large, curved metal tool from his tool box and headed for the back door.

"Oh, I hate to take you away from what you're doing but . . . *thank you*!" I said with almost a squeal, and hurried to keep up with him.

"My pleasure."

The yard was overgrown with weeds. There were signs that there had once been a path to the cottage, which was a distance behind the house and overgrown with ivy. "Have you ever been in there?" I tried not to sound too anxious.

"Not since I was a kid. We'd sneak here in the middle of the night and tell scary stories. Great memories."

"Did you grow up around here, then?"

"My grandmother lived in town. I spent the summers with her because my mom worked. Not sure anyone's been in here in years. Got your flashlight?"

"Sure, flashlight and a knife, what more could a girl need?" I teased.

"A knife?"

"My grandfather was a whittler and taught me when I was young," I said. "Life with my parents was always strict and proper. I loved visiting my grandparents because it was laid back, sitting on the front porch carving small animals and boats." I chattered while we headed through the overgrowth. "My grandfather gave me a pearl-handled knife for my seventh birthday when he deemed me proficient. A lot of women carry lipstick, I carry a knife. He made sure I could use it as a tool or a weapon. It comes in handy."

I pulled it from my pocket and showed him. He looked from my knife to my eyes, then pulled out his own knife, slightly larger but otherwise identical. "Yours looks a little more worn than mine," he said quietly.

Wondering if he'd noticed my pounding pulse, I said, "I haven't carved in over a decade. Maybe things will be slow enough I'll be able to hone my skills. And it looks like I have plenty of room to do target practice with it."

"You've got your work cut out for you in the house for a while, but make sure you give us plenty of warning before you polish your rusty target skills," he said, smiling.

The vines pulled away easily from the door and he cut down years of growth to clear our path. While he tried several keys, I observed him in an objective manner. Chiseled chin, dark hair that would make most women jealous, muscular, competent, at least six feet or a little more, but it was the snapping of the old bolt that seriously accelerated my heart.

"Ready?" he asked, pulling a flashlight from his back pocket. The sturdy door creaked from years of neglect, and it took a moment for my eyes to adjust to the dim light.

Unconsciously I put my hand on his back as I tiptoed in. The house was larger than I expected, and darker. He cleared cobwebs as we made our way into the front room, shining light into corners and around the room.

"Wait here," he said.

"Not on your life."

"Then aim the light on the window to your left."

He pulled the metal tool from his pocket and dislodged a corner. With the strain of old nails breaking free of wood that had long been their resting place, the plywood cover released its grip with a groan. The room filled with an eerie light, filtered through dust and a vine-covered window. Furniture was covered with dusty white sheets. I felt like I'd stepped back in time and didn't want words to break the spell.

There was enough light now that Brandan could make his way across the room to relieve the other windows of coverings that had protected them for decades. Even with vines covering them, sunlight poured through to illuminate the room in a peculiar hue. My enthusiasm grew with the anticipation of revealing the long-boarded fireplace. He removed the plywood in one pull. Milky greens and smoky turquoise blues, the fireplace was magnificent. I knew I would spend hours studying it.

"Is that a Van Briggle?" I asked reverently, having some knowledge of the famous turn-of-the-Century potter who had come to Colorado to find a cure for his tuberculosis.

"It is indeed. I'm impressed, Counselor. Bring your flashlight," he said in a low tone, making his way into the next room.

Following closely, we found a small but complete kitchen. When Brandan pulled a board from the left side of the room, it exposed a doorway that obviously went outside. "Plenty of time to get that one open later." His voice was low, as though he was as aware as I of the reverent discovery we were sharing. In each room we entered, he pried plywood from portals, bringing to life a place that had long lain dormant.

There were two bedrooms, one on either side of the back of the house, with random pieces of furniture covered with cloths. The bathroom between them had a clawfoot tub and a doorway into each of the rooms. "Do you feel like we just found buried treasure?"

He gave me a smile. "There's enough to keep you busy out here for a long time," he said with a slight strain as he pulled the last of the wood.

"Can you believe this? Do you come across stuff like this often? I'm so enchanted," I said in the solemn voice that felt appropriate.

"I have to admit this is a first even for me. We come across unusual situations, but this has been sealed long enough, no telling what you'll find."

"When the time's right, I'll spend hours learning its secrets. But I think it's more important to get the main house operational first. It feels like it'll take years to do everything that needs to be done just to make it livable."

"Not quite that long, but that's a wise choice. This place isn't going anywhere."

"Thank you for understanding. This is an alteration in time for me, but it's still amazing. I make my living talking, but I don't seem to be able to find any words to explain how it's affecting me. So . . . thanks for taking the time to show me. I'll lock up."

"No problem." He paused, "By the way, I'm sure we haven't, but I'd mentioned to Miles earlier that I felt like we'd met before, so I was surprised when you said it."

He headed back to the house. The last thing I wanted or needed was to be aware of him as a man. That was a path I had no intention of taking.

CHAPTER 4

"You're not supposed to go in there. My Mama says you'll get in lotsa trouble if you do," I heard a child's voice say as I locked the padlock.

"Thank you for letting me know. Your Mama's a smart woman. I'm the new owner. I'm gonna make it pretty again. What's your name?"

The precocious tow-headed boy appeared to be about five, and his enormous blue eyes melted my heart. "I'm James Gabriel, what's your name?"

"My name's Jordan. Do you live nearby?"

"I have a cousin named Jordan, only he's a boy. How come you have a boy's name?"

"It's a name for either boys or girls. Some names are like that. But your names are for a boy. How old are you?"

"I'm six and a half and I'm in first grade. How old are you?"

"I'm thirty two," I said, leaning so I was more on his level.

"What grade are you in?" he said matter of factly.

"I'm not in school any more. I went for a long time, and now I'm a lawyer in New York. I'm here for a while because my aunt died and gave me this house."

"My dad died before my baby brother was born. He's almost a year now. His name's Caden."

Just then a woman's voice could be heard in the distance. "I gotta go. Mama gets upset when I don't come right away when she calls."

"Will you come back and see me sometime if it's okay with your mom?"

"Will you let me look inside the old lady's house?"

"Sure," I said to his retreating back.

There were ten acres that sloped gently up the mountainside. I wandered through some of the open fields and patches of trees, and sometime soon I'd have someone show me the property lines. As I came in the back door, I was thinking of my encounter outside the cottage. "Either of you know James Gabriel? Or more specifically, what happened to his dad?"

"Ah, so you met the young James. Awful situation," Brandan said. "Good provider, good dad. Teenage boys were playing on the frozen Reservoir. Ice wasn't thick enough and they fell in. Gabe was driving by. He was able to get both of them out but couldn't get out himself. Cold water takes you fast. Finally got him, but he died on the way to the hospital. April was pregnant with their second. The town rallied and they want for nothing, but it was tragic."

"He seems like a precious child."

Miles and Brandan shared a smile. "Precious he may be," said Miles, "but he'll talk your ear off."

"I can see that," I said, covering a yawn. "Can't understand why I'm so tired. It's not even noon."

"It's the altitude," Brandan said. "We're higher than most, and you're coming from sea level. It'll take a day or two to acclimate, maybe more. And you'll most likely get headaches, so be prepared. Drink lots of water, rest, you'll be fine."

"Thanks! Don't worry about me with the noise, do what needs to be done. I'm gonna read and maybe sleep some of this off."

"We'll be here," Miles said, pulling wire through plaster.

❧❧❧

Each of the rooms on the second floor took on its own appeal. I visualized them without their dingy wallpaper and worn carpet. I spent time in each one, mentally decorating, wondering at previous lives that had taken place inside these walls. I imagined the space becoming modern and inviting while retaining its vintage charm. I saw potential, and the lives that would be shared here. The house felt alive; I wanted to know it.

I was again drawn to the turret room. Light rays played off dust particles that hung lightly in the air. I could see the water clearly and thought of the tragedy of James Gabriel's father, and prayed that as he grew older there might be solace for him that his father died a hero.

Several times I tried to open the armoire. I sat on the floor facing it, wondering what treasures it might hold. It was too heavy to move. Maybe there was a key, maybe there was a tool that would work the lock. I was tired and the warmth of the sun felt good beating down on my weary body. I was only going to be there for a few moments.

"Jordan. Wake up." Brandan gently touched my shoulder. "Wake up or you're gonna be sore." The sun had almost disappeared. "Miles and I are leaving. I wanted to make sure you weren't up here without a flashlight."

"Oh! I can't believe I slept that long. And you're right. My neck *is* sore."

"We'll see you in the morning. Anything you need before I go?"

"No, I'm good. *Wait!* Yes! There *is* a favor I'd like to ask. Do you know if there's a key to the closet? I know it must've been locked forever, but I wondered if your magic key ring might have the appropriate tool attached."

"I'll be right back."

Back in under a minute, he tried each key to no avail. "Sorry, Jordan, we'll have to figure something else out. None of these will do the trick. I'll see if I can open it tomorrow."

"Seriously? You're just gonna leave me like this?"

"Um, what did you have in mind?"

"Don't tease. Can you honestly walk out and not want to know what's in there? Is it only me who'll stay up all night trying to figure out how to open it?"

His smile took hold. "I'll be right back."

I had the formidable task of holding the flashlight. After several minutes of listening and tinkering, the rusted metal let loose of its clasped hold and the doors to the antique quarter-sawn oak closet groaned. "You do the honors," Brandan said, almost reverently. There were dust-covered sheets wrapped around something, along with two large leather duffel bags. "Do you want me to take them out and set them on the floor?"

"Yes, please."

I was surprised by his gentleness as he slid his arms under the stack of what appeared to be clothing and set it ever-so-carefully on the worn oak planks. When everything was out, he said, "I'll hold the flashlight now. Let's see what you found."

Inside were beautiful gowns with sequins, lace, satin, and fur. They appeared to be circa 1920s to 1940s, and were beautifully preserved. "Any idea who these might have belonged to?" I asked.

"No, the house has been vacant for almost three decades, so no telling where they came from. Did you know the aunt who left you the house?"

"Not well. I remember her from when I was a kid. My mom had two sisters. Agnes died when she was two. Madeline, the one who owned this house, never married and never had children. She was in a horrible car accident when she was in her early thirties, and was in a nursing home the rest of her life. My mother wasn't able to take care of her, and I only remember seeing her once after that when I was about fourteen."

Brandan sat on the floor next to me and continued to hold the flashlight. "I know it adds an eerie feel with direct light in the darkness, but it'll give you an idea."

The beam reflected off cut crystals, illuminated the silky sheen of the material, and defined individual strands of fur at a collar or cuff. "Aren't they beautiful?" I asked in awe, gently setting each of them aside.

When there was no answer, I tried to focus on him behind the light, then laughed. "Yeah, this must be thrilling. Old dresses in an empty attic with a crazy stranger who's covered in dirt from sleeping the afternoon away on the bare floor. Exciting times, indeed."

Softly, he said, "The fun is in watching your enjoyment."

"Thank you." I hoped he couldn't see me blush as I realized the intimacy of our setting.

"It's nice to see through new eyes," he said. "I tend to be jaded with the familiar. It's enjoyable to see the simple become profound, that's all."

They were handsome treasures, and I would preserve as much of their integrity as possible. Looking at the last of the gowns, I thanked him for his indulgence. One of the flashlights stood on end, adding shadows and light to the floor-to-ceiling bookcase. His silhouette played eerily. "Now I have a more practical question for you. I'd love to connect this room to the other room on this level. Do you think structurally it'll be possible to open one to the other?"

"If you can dream it, there's not much that's not possible."

"When you're finished with the electrical, can we talk about what can be done, and what should or shouldn't be done? I'd like your counsel on what *you* think we should do. I need practical input, then I'll dream."

"Miles and I should be finished tomorrow, then I'll brainstorm with you. You should be able to take a warm shower in about thirty-six hours."

"I discovered this morning that if you're tired, there's nothing like ice water coming out of the pipes at almost nine thousand feet above sea level to get your creative juices flowing."

"Give me hot water any day," he said. "Do you want to follow me down?"

"Good heavens, yes. I'm adventurous, just not that brave yet. Give me a couple of days."

CHAPTER 5

The freezing shower wasn't something I'd want to get used to, but there was no doubt it got the blood pumping in the morning. The sawing and hammering continued downstairs, so I headed in the other direction with design elements in mind.

Andrew would have hated it here. Dusty, dirty, unfinished, cold water—he would have been complaining the moment we pulled into the drive. I shuddered at what a close call I'd had, and would never question my decision. I had no answers, only questions, but I didn't care what the answers were. I was glad to be away from prying eyes, and was surprisingly numb over his betrayal. The initial anger had given way to relief and indifference.

I knew I'd have to call Jeni soon. We'd been texting, but I explained that cell reception was sporadic. The real reason was that I didn't want that life intruding here. I would have to smooth things over with Father, too. He exploded when I told him the news. I was grateful his anger had been directed at Andrew, not me. I had only minor guilt that I'd left them to handle the fallout.

The bookcase would go in the office once the pass-through was opened. It was frustrating when it wouldn't budge. I sat on the ground and tried to lever it with my feet, used my shoulder to push, tried to pull it from the wall, nothing worked. I was in excellent physical condition and had no intention of being bested by a bookcase.

Sunlight played through swaying trees, giving the tiger-striped oak an almost sinister movement. On either side was carved molding. There were no nail holes to indicate where it was attached, but it seemed logical it was screwed to the wall.

Heading to kitchen for tools, a petite brunette was talking to Miles and Brandan. "Hey, Jordan," Miles said with an exaggerated smile. "Come meet April."

As I crossed the room to shake her hand, she said, "You must be the lawyer lady James Gabriel was talkin' about. Nice to meet you."

"Oh, are you his mom? What a darling young man! So polite."

"Thank you. I'm working on it."

"You're doing a great job."

"April came to bring us food," Miles said with a wink to Brandan.

"That was nice of you." I wondered if I'd missed something when I saw the look that passed between the men.

"No trouble at all. I wanted to see what they were doing at the old Stratton place, and my mom's visiting so it was a good time to slip over."

"It's a mess, but feel free to look around."

"Thanks. I need to be getting back. Maybe some other time?" she asked, looking directly at Brandan.

Not sure which of us was supposed to answer, I saw her face fall when he walked out of the room. Miles was smiling, and I tried to cover the awkward moment with, "Sure, come up any time. I'd love to see James Gabriel again and meet Caden."

Turning to Miles, she said, "You gonna be working here long?"

"I'll be done today. Brandan and his crew will be here after Jordan and Brandan decide what needs to be done."

"Thanks for the food." I tried to break what felt like tension.

She seemed almost dejected. "I'm sure I'll see you around."

I didn't know what was going on, I'm not sure I cared. It would be easier not to get involved with these people if I wasn't going to be staying. Heading into the parlor where Brandan was working, I asked if I could use a screwdriver. "Sure. Slotted or Phillips? Big or little?"

"I have no idea."

"I'll find something that'll work," he said.

I overheard Miles say to him, "Maybe one of these days she'll get the message, huh?" so I was surprised when Brandan was immediately back.

"The tips are magnetic and interchangeable so you should have any size you need. If the screws are old, let me know and I'll drill them out." He went back to pulling wires through walls. I felt like I was sneaking as I closed the door to the turret room behind me.

Even though this was out of my usual realm, there was an allure to finding a solution. How difficult could it be? I sat on the floor and removed the lowest shelf, thinking there may be screws behind it. Nothing. Setting it aside, I repeated the process with the second shelf with the same results. There had to be a logical explanation.

Standing to get the proper angle, the entire bookshelf pivoted as I lifted the middle shelf. Slowly, silently, the right side of the case shifted away from me, the other moving toward me. I jumped out of the way, heart hammering, having no clue what had happened. When it was perpendicular with the opening, it stopped.

It was so unexpected I didn't move. The thumping of my heart was deafening. I was half-expecting the guys to come running, half expecting someone to step out of the murky shadows. With quivering hands I aimed the flashlight into the darkness. It was a room, no more than four feet deep.

Inching forward, I grasped my light as though it was a weapon. In a sense, it was protection from the darkness that was somehow terrifying. I ran light across the floor, up the walls, across the ceiling. Nothing was visible except years of dust and cobwebs. The walls were dark, covered in wainscoting.

I stepped in slowly, creeping along the wall behind me, pulse pounding, shining the light around the door that extended half way into the room. The entire room appeared to be about twelve feet long. Dusty bugs hung lifelessly from sagging webs. On the far end was a wooden bench. Making sure nothing was in my path, it was the matching bench to the downstairs piano. There were no light fixtures, and nothing appeared to have been disturbed in years.

"Hey, Jordan, want something to eat?" I heard Brandan call from downstairs.

Did anyone else know about this? My nerves strung out, I knew I couldn't sit calmly or act normally right now. Slipping into the main room, I gently pushed on the pivoting case. It returned silently into the wall. Going to the door, afraid he might come upstairs, I tried to sound as normal as possible.

"I'll be down in a while, thanks. I'm exploring."

"There's plenty to eat when you're ready."

"Thank you."

Hearing him walk away, I hoped the entry would again reveal its secret. Lifting ever so slightly, it swung soundlessly open. The sun was shining, but there were places so dark as to be black. A movement next to me almost produced a scream, until I saw it was shadows playing through the outside trees. Breathing again, I ran the flashlight over the walls, noting the care someone had taken to design the room and make it undiscoverable. Shifting the light, something reflected. I approached with trepidation.

A hinge ran the length of the right corner. I searched for a handle on the left side of the short wall, but there wasn't one. The hinges had to have a reason, and I intended to find out. Nothing marred the perfection of the wall except one knothole just above eye level. Was I missing something?

On a whim, I gingerly stuck my finger in the hole and pulled, and for the second time that day my heart felt as though it would leave my chest. A door opened, although not as silently, and again I waited to see if anyone heard. A room in a room in a home in the middle of nowhere. You can't make this stuff up, and I wished Jeni was here. She would have blazed ahead and made it boisterous, not terrifying.

Did I want to get Brandan before I went further? What if there were bones or creatures? If anything was here, it wouldn't still be alive, I reasoned. *Get yourself under control, Jordan. What's the worst that can happen?*

On the floor stood a large chest, thigh high and approximately three feet long, like an oversized hope chest. Was the room built to the size of the chest, or the chest made to fit this space? I would never know, but I felt like Pandora.

There was a brass clasp on the front, secured by a sturdy lock. It appeared to require a skeleton key. The old hinges were quieter as I stepped out and closed the bookcase. I was frustrated when I walked into the kitchen to find Miles, Brandan, and Jack standing in front of the coveted drawer that held the keyring.

"Hey, how are you liking our little town?"

"Hi, Jack, nice to see you," I said, extending my hand. "Haven't seen much of it. Spent most of my time exploring the house and grounds and trying to adjust to the altitude."

"Yeah, it'll get you if you're not used to it, that's for sure. Callie should be by tomorrow. She's been back and forth to Denver this week so she hasn't had much time."

"No worries. I'm not going anywhere for a while." Was I truthfully standing here carrying on a normal conversation?

"Everything is finished that needs to be done for tomorrow. The City will be out to check and flip the switch to give you electricity. If you're ready to get to work, we can supply the crew. Brandan will be around for the next few days, so talk it over and figure out what you want done."

"I'm overwhelmed with your kindness."

"One of the benefits and drawbacks of a small town, we take care of each other."

"Yeah, just like Manhattan," I said with humorous sarcasm.

"I can only imagine," Jack said.

"If you'll excuse me, I'd like to get the keys out of the drawer." I extended my hand to Miles. "Thanks so much for your help. I hope to see you around often. My goal is to make this a working Bed and Breakfast, and I make wicked stuffed French toast. Stop by any time."

"You and Callie can compare notes. She makes the best pumpkin pecan pancakes this side of the Mississippi," Jack laughed.

"It'll be fun having someone to share ideas with."

"Take care of yourself," said Miles. "I'll be here helping when I can. I live over the hill in Sugarloaf, so I'm not too far away if you ever need anything. Not that you will with these brutes around, but don't hesitate."

"I won't forget. Excuse me."

They moved away from the drawer and continued talking as I got the keys. There didn't appear to be skeleton keys, but I didn't want to look like I was on a mission, so I left the room casually. "Thanks, again. See you soon," I called over my shoulder, then ran.

CHAPTER 6

Heart racing, it was easy now that I knew what I was doing. It swung silently open, as did the door that hid the chest. I would put a lamp in here when the electricity came on to dispel the sinister shadows. It wasn't worth trying, none of the keys would fit. I could see the headlines now, "New York Lawyer found babbling in a closet in a rundown, hundred-year-old home." I had to get out of here.

Brandan knew the house well, and might have something that would open the lock. He was alone in the kitchen, cleaning up debris. "You look like you've seen a ghost."

I felt unsteady. "Are there skeleton keys around?"

"I don't know what I thought you were going to say, but that wouldn't have been on the list," he laughed. "You okay?"

"We need to talk."

"Sounds serious. You decide you don't want electricity?" He smiled.

I was so distracted, it took a minute to register. "Oh, sorry. Brandan . . ."

"You find the body?"

"Maybe." *That* got his attention.

"*What*? I was kidding. I hope you are too."

"Come on."

I held the door to the turret room until he was in, then closed it. "You trying to keep someone out?" he asked, clearly puzzled.

"Brandan, I need your help."

Seeing the intensity on my face, he said, "What do you need?"

Trying to read him, we stood staring. I felt like our lives were about to change, but maybe I was being overly dramatic. "We don't know each other well, but I feel I can trust you. I have to be able to trust you. I won't insult you by asking you to keep this a secret, but I'm about to explode and can't do this by myself."

"Tell me," he said, holding my gaze.

I barely lifted the middle shelf and the unit rotated. I saw the surprise on his face. We looked at each other. I pulled the flashlight out of my pocket and handed it to him, then picked up the larger one lying on the floor inside the hidden room. Turning them on, we looked around the room, and I could see he was looking at it as I had earlier. I gave him time to absorb before I hit him with the next shock.

"In all my years, I've never seen anything like it. How'd you find it?" he asked as he continued to look around.

"I wanted to move the bookcase, so I took the shelves out. When I got to the middle shelf, it activated something. Someday you can tell me how it works, but that's not important right now."

"No, just finding this is pretty amazing. What do you suppose it was used for?"

"There's more," I said in a whisper.

"Okay." I loved that he wasn't ruffled.

"This is why I need your help," I said as I pulled gently on the door. I watched him and wondered if his heart was thumping as mine had. He looked unaffected, but I knew he couldn't be. Nothing moved on his body except his eyes which turned toward me. "How could you have come down so composed knowing this was here? I'm impressed."

I stood next to him, holding the flashlight, peering into the long-lost confines. I touched his arm as I got closer. He whistled when he saw the chest. Seeming to come out of the spell, he crouched to examine the lock. "There are skeleton keys hanging in the pantry. Will you be okay for a minute?"

"*Hurry.*"

A few minutes later, he grinned and said, "These locks were made to keep honest people out, so don't judge me." He listened intently until the metal gave way and we stared at each other. "Be my guest."

"No, I'll stand behind you and watch like a chicken."

He removed the lock and opened the hinge. "Ready?"

I held the light. Across the top, folded neatly, was a quilt. I was again impressed by how gentle, almost protective, a tough-guy like Brandan was in lifting one quilt and then another as he stepped into the fading light of the turret room. "Do you want these up here or in your room?"

"Is there a place in the armoire to set them? Until we have time to examine them, I hate to put them on the floor."

"Do you want to look at these? We can save the rest for later."

"You're kidding, right? There's no way I could walk away. I want to know what required such a secret hiding place."

"I don't mean to sound fanciful" he said quietly, "but I feel like this is going to be a pivotal point, and everything as we know it is about to change. Easy to understand how Pandora got into trouble."

"I thought the same thing earlier."

Our eyes met in the shadowy light. In a soft voice, I said, "Someone went to a lot of trouble to make sure that whatever's in here stayed safe. We can learn from the past, so if *you're* ready, *I* am."

"I'm going to start calling you Digger. Are you always this tenacious?" He gave me a friendly hug. I felt like he was sharing his strength.

"Usually. I love following trails to logical conclusions."

There was an untarnished metal box with a small locking mechanism. "I know someone who can open this. Do you want me to set this on the floor in the other room?"

"Yes, please. We'll make sure this room stays locked while we filter through what's here. Unless there are others around who have your talent for picking locks?" I asked in jest. Everything seemed sinister with the unnatural light of the flashlights that stood on end and fanned across the ceiling.

"Do you want more light?"

"No, quite frankly, I don't want you to leave me right now. I feel like I broke into someone's house and I'm about to get caught."

"I understand. What else is there?"

"Two metal boxes. Oh, my God, what appears to be a journal, a large wooden box and, hmmm, let me see, two more quilts," I handed everything to him one by one.

"Looks like we both have our work cut out for us. If it's all right with you, I'll play locksmith in the morning.

CHAPTER 7

There was a certain reverence required in opening the journal. The penmanship was exquisite in classic turn-of-the-century perfection. The inside cover indicated it belonged to Edward J. Stratton. Every nerve in my body tightened as I read the first words. I must have made a sound because Brandan was beside me in an instant. "What is it?"

"Remember that part about our lives not being the same after this? You weren't far off." Stunned, I handed him the book.

"Our first week together in our new home has left me filled with awe at your strength, my beautiful Jordan," he read aloud. *"I never knew life could be as complete as it is when you share it with someone you love."*

In the dim light of the turret room, Brandan closed the book. "I'm not sure what any of it means, or even if it will come to have any significance, but I want you to know, whatever happens, I'm here. The deeper we dig into the trunk, the more of an impact it will have. You don't have to face it alone."

"It's obviously uncharted waters for both of us, Brand, and I appreciate that. Jordan must be an ancestor. Hopefully we'll find answers."

"I'm not sure you're aware you're doing it, but I like it when you call me Brand," he said, closing the passage to the hidden room.

Smiling at each other in the unnatural light, I said, "That's a good thing then, huh? It'd be a shame if I was annoying you from the start. On the other hand, I feel like we're old friends."

"Me too," he said softly. "It must have been such a different life to live without electricity. I suppose when you don't know what you're missing, it's one thing, but I see how these old houses are built and they didn't have power tools at the time – it's pretty impressive."

"It hasn't been horrid, but I wouldn't want to live this way for long."

"Regional will be here in the morning, then the utility company, so you should be all set no later than noon. I know you're excited about the find and I don't want to take you away from it, but maybe tomorrow we can go room to room and get ideas about what you want done so I can plan the work crew? If we get started, we can have it finished by Halloween."

"Do you think these should go back to their hiding place for the night?"

"No, they'll be fine here, I promise. We'll lock the door and no one else will be in the house tonight. You staying here or coming downstairs?"

"Much as I'm anxious to look, I'm exhausted. And I've done enough research over the years to know it'll take months to filter through it all. Do you know if one of your keys works in the door?"

"We'll find one that does, trust me, or I personally know someone who can make it secure," he said, pulling out the ring and trying them. Half way through he said, "That was it. Ready?"

His flashlight illuminated the stairs. "You okay?"

"Reading that affected me strangely. I felt like he was talking to me when I first read it."

"I can see that. It'll be interesting to learn about him."

Brandan stopped on his way to the front door. "Your whole life is upside down. The culture shock of leaving Manhattan, coming to Nederland, staying here with no

electricity, then to encounter what you did today, you
have to be on sensory overload."

"I'll either sleep like the dead or not be able to sleep
at all."

"Here's my number. Call if you need me for
anything. I'm not far away."

"Thank you. I can't wait to get some electricity in
this place. The past few days have made me appreciate
what I have. Who knew there would come a time I
would be so thankful for something so simple?"

"When this house was built, it was in the middle of
nowhere. The reservoir wouldn't be here for over a
decade, no electricity, no indoor plumbing. Women
wore long dresses with no washing machines, and no
neighbors for miles. It's certainly changed since
Edward wrote in his journal."

"I can't wait to read it. I'm usually up before the
sun, so if you want to head up early, we can talk about
plans."

�֍ ✤ ✤ ✤

"Compliments of Sam down at the Amber Rose,"
Brandan said as he set the bag on the counter early
the next morning. "He's a great cook and will be a good
ally for you. And Callie will be up around noon. She
does a lot of decorating and staging, so she'll help if
you want."

"I can trick out a New York condo with the best of
'em, but I'm not too familiar with Victorians. I'd
appreciate her help. And you're out of luck this
morning. I can't find the fine china to serve you."

"Sam sent plates and silverware, said to bring 'em
back when you're set up. No hurry."

"I'm not used to such friendliness. I could get used
to it."

"You'll have to earn your respect with a lot of them,
but they take care of their own. Considering you

inherited from your Aunt Madeline whom many of them knew, you shouldn't have too much trouble."

"Did you know her?"

"No. I was a kid when she left. We used to have parties on the grounds when I was in high school, far enough away from anyone so we were pretty much left alone."

"Small towns. I went to prep school, then Cornell, then their law school. My father didn't take kindly to parties at any point along the way since he always wanted me to be the best, and frivolities didn't get you there, or so he said on more than one occasion."

"And were you the best?"

"Nah. I was mediocre to one of the foremost legal minds on Wall Street. I've spent every day since I graduated working to make him proud. In fairness, I've come a long way to redemption."

"That's a lot to live up to," he said, resting his hand on mine. His concern was touching, and I wondered if he was offering more than comfort. It had been a long time since I'd felt butterflies at a man's touch, but it didn't matter, it wasn't going to happen.

"No worries. It made me the person I am today. Shall we start with the main floor? We have enough light. Can I draw you the floor plan I have in mind?"

"I have sophisticated software that will show you exactly what it'll look like and allow you to change dimensions, colors, placement. Not much we can't do."

We worked companionably for half an hour, Brandan having excellent input and options. I was able to see the finished product and feel the life that would take place here. We moved into the dining room. Like the rest of the house, the oak trim around the doors and windows had been spared the painter's brush and should clean up nicely. I loved the swinging door to the kitchen, the light fixture appeared to be original, and I'd have Callie help me pick colors.

There was intricate fretwork and a fireplace that had unusual tile. "And that's not a Van Briggle, correct?"

"Correct, it predates his work by about a decade. This was probably imported from Europe, a popular custom at the time. And I've been meaning to ask you about the tiny ice skates you put on the mantle. There's apparently some significance. Were they yours?"

"I wore them as a young child, but have no idea where they came from. My mother had them when she was little. There's something about them that's touched my heart from my earliest memories."

"I can see that."

"A friend of mine lost everything in a fire. For a long time I wondered what I would take if I only had five minutes to get out in similar circumstances, and the skates were one of the first things that came to mind. I sold a co-op in the City recently and put some things in storage. I couldn't bear to leave these locked away, so I brought them." I blushed at how silly that must sound. "I suppose we all have our own neuroses, huh?"

"Not neurotic at all. They're distinctive."

"That's kind of you to say. I may put them in a shadow box and leave them on display in here. They feel like they've come home." We looked at each other. "Okay, now I just sound nuts. Let's get on with this." I laughed, but Brandan studied me as we moved to the next room.

CHAPTER 8

From the entry there was a doorway to the dining room and one to what was probably originally the parlor. It seemed strange they were separate rooms that didn't open into each other. Both were elegant. Getting rid of the out-dated, depressing wallpaper would be one of my first projects.

"I want a sitting room, gathering place. It's large and I envision different seating areas. Can we put French doors to the wraparound porch? It seems a shame not to have access."

"Great idea and simple enough. Shouldn't take long to get that done."

"Any idea where we can put a powder room?"

"The space under the stairs has direct plumbing access from the basement and the second floor. You could turn that into a usable area."

"I *love* that idea! I have intriguing plans for themes for each room. If I were doing something besides law, I always thought I'd run a unique coffee shop in Manhattan with separate areas, each decorated with a different ambiance. Might as well use the idea here."

"Then give me your vision so I can see it, too, and I'll do what I can to make it your reality." My heart contracted at his words.

Everyone showed up at once—Regional Building, the utility company, Callie. It was enjoyable confusion. When the utilities came on, the lights and whirring motors and ceiling fans started at once. Brandan and I exchanged a look, knowing we were both thinking of our upstairs discovery. He flashed me a grin.

"I'm gonna go through the house and check the rooms, make sure lights are working and that nothing's out of place. Here's the note pad. Jot down ideas and I'll be back," he said, taking the stairs two at a time.

I shared my design ideas with Callie. We'd made it through the first two rooms when she said, "Okay, it's none of my business, but did I see something special going on between you two?"

"Hardly," I said with a laugh. "But your frankness is refreshing. Not much I appreciate more than honesty, even in my business. I love the shock value of truth, so I appreciate you asking. But I'm not looking for an entanglement. I don't plan on being here long, and I'm not too keen on relationships right now."

"Sounds like heartache on the other side of *that* statement. We'll talk about that sometime, but I'm glad there's nothing starting. Brandan is one of my all-time favorite people. He's worked for Jack for years, and Jack puts a lot of stock in him, which says a lot. But he's not a man that a woman wants to lose her heart to. He'll break it."

"I overheard him and Miles talking about April. I have to admit I was curious."

"Oh, poor April. It was tragic about Gabe. That happened right before I got here. Brandan is a wonderful comforter and was trying to help out. He and Gabe were friends, and Brandan tried to help his widow, no more, no less. She thought there was more being offered. She was pregnant and alone with a little boy, and she was scared. Brandan was familiar, comfortable. I'm surprised they were talking about it now, though. It's been a while."

"Doesn't seem to be so for April. She came up yesterday."

"That's too bad. Brandan is a strange combination of huge heart and no heart. He'd do anything for anyone except stick around after they say 'I love you.' He's not gonna let anyone catch him, and avoids entanglements at all costs. I've always hoped someone would help him settle down, but I'll be surprised if that happens."

"That's good insight, but not really my concern."

"What's not your concern?" Brandan said from the doorway.

"What the place was called before," I responded. "I'm gonna rename it. What do you think of Madeline Manor after my aunt?"

"I think that's wonderful!" said Callie. "What a nice tribute. And the people who are left who knew her are the ones it'll be important to. That's a perfect idea!"

I was pleased she had joined us. Her insights were excellent. My upstairs lair would be called Willow Tree. Each room would have its own bath, and four of the five rooms were large enough to have a soaking tub as well as a shower. Three of the rooms already had a closet, and I would put armoires in the two that didn't. The Inn was going to be a thing of beauty when we were done.

"Here's something I've been thinking about," I said as we headed down the stairs. "Do either of you have suggestions about the outside color other than the depressing gun-metal gray that's there?"

"I see it in a pale green," Callie said.

"You ladies tell me colors, we'll get it done. But if you're not too familiar with Victorians, Jordan, it's the third color that makes it pop. So a main color and a trim color, and you have all of the fish-scale highlights on the third floor that can draw out the structure. I put my vote in for blues."

"I've stood outside several times and looked at it from all angles and tried to get a feeling for it. I keep coming back to yellow—kind of a butter yellow with green highlights. But we don't have to decide today. Is there anything else, Brandan?"

"Let's talk about the roof," he said as we wandered around the building. When we were done, Callie hugged me and told me she'd be back in a few days to see how things were progressing, and to call if I needed anything.

As she pulled away, Brandan said, "I'm proud of you. I bet you play a mean game of poker. Hell, I'd want you on my side in a courtroom, that's for sure."

"What do you mean?"

"There's nothing in your outward appearance to indicate you're itching to get back to the attic. I'm fascinated with what might be up there, so you have to be chompin' at the bit."

"I will admit I found myself mentally drifting to the attic on more than one occasion." I said with a wink. "Race you?"

We took off for the porch in a dead heat. Brandan's legs may have been longer, but I've been running for years, so he was surprised when I beat him to the front door. "Drat," I said at the foot of the staircase, "we forgot the basement. Is there a light down there? Can we look now so we're finished?"

"Sure, and we have enough flashlights if there's not."

"Here's what I'm thinking. Give me your opinion and tell me if it's possible. I don't plan on being here long, but I'll want to come back often. Willow Tree is mine," I said as we exchanged a look of understanding. "I don't want anyone up there but you."

"I like the way you think, Counselor," he said with a raised brow.

"Stop, you know what I mean." I laughed. "I want an Innkeeper who'll stay on the grounds during the off season. I want to make an inviting place to live down here so we don't lose any of the upstairs rooms. Not sure they need a full kitchen, but a bedroom, bath, living room, private laundry, kitchenette, is there room for all that?"

We checked out the stone foundation for stability and talked about the kind of lighting we'd need to make it feel cheerful. "There's enough room you could put a second bedroom if you're so inclined. You've got plenty of room. We need to figure out the mechanical room, and you can use as much of the rest of the space as you'd like."

We headed to the stairs that led to the kitchen. "If possible, I'd also like to open the outside entrance that's been covered over so the lower level is self-sustaining."

"Regional Building will make us do that anyway, so when I bring my laptop you can tell me what appeals."

"Speaking of laptops! I've been so out of touch with reality. I live on my computer and haven't had internet, or electricity to charge the battery. Strange that I don't care. The rest of the world could be in chaos, and I wouldn't even know."

"I assure you, the rest of the world *is* in chaos, that's why we live up here. It's a town where hippies grow old. Very laid back.

CHAPTER 9

"Are we dancing around the inevitable, Brand?"

He looked at me with some surprise and smiled. "You don't have to ask me twice."

Realizing what he must have heard, I laughed. "Stop it. I'm talking about the attic."

"I knew that, but just to set your mind at ease, I've never seduced a client."

"So formal, but I guess that's what I am, huh? Shoe's on the other foot now."

"Want to be something else?"

"No wonder women have a hard time with your charm. But since we're having this discussion, let's lay our cards on the table. I'm not gonna be one of them. I'm not vulnerable to pretty words and a handsome face."

"For a lawyer lady, I'd think you'd know better than to throw down such a challenge."

I laughed. "You're hopeless, mister. The last thing I need in my life right now is a one-night stand. Heaven forbid. You're attractive, no one's gonna deny that. I've felt a strange connection to you since the beginning, but let's leave it right there. Nothing's gonna happen. Not now. So let's share this unique experience and see where it leads."

"What makes you think it would only be one night?" he said, stepping closer.

"Sorry, Brand, your reputation preceded you." Was I breathless?

"All teasing aside," he said, "we have a lot of work to do together. We've laid the cards on the table, and there's no question there's an attraction, and an undeniable connection for both of us. But you and I are gonna be in the thick of it. A lot of marriages don't survive what we're getting ready to face with this remodel, so we both need to be able to roll with the punches."

"It *will* be a lot, won't it?"

"Absolutely, and I wasn't kidding when I said I don't get involved with clients. You and I are gonna be good friends. We're gonna have an unusual amount of trust between us. Hell, we already do. We've shared some interesting experiences in just a few days."

"There's no doubt there'll be a lot more before we're done, so I appreciate the frankness. I'm not in the mood to trust people. The fact that I like you and trust you says a lot. What next?"

"Since the overhead light is working in your room, why don't we take the lamps to the turret room? I'll get it set up so you can explore to your heart's content. I'll give you some space and get things done around here that you'll need, like making sure the water heater's working and getting your cable going and . . . What?"

"I want you to know I appreciate you and your efforts. You've been a wonderful buffer between me and harsh reality, and I recognize you're the one that made it happen. Thank you."

"My pleasure," he said. "Let's get you situated."

Brandan positioned the lamps to reach into the darkness of the secret room. It was much larger than I thought, and the wood was well preserved. "Is it oak?" I asked with a degree of reverence.

"Yeah, and except for the knothole you so cleverly found, it's perfect."

"I'm a relatively savvy woman, but my insides are jumping up and down like a kid."

"Then I'll leave you to it. I'll be back to check on you in a bit."

"Thanks. I won't be leaving here for a while, I'm sure."

With a delicious kind of fear, I picked up the leather-bound journal we'd found the night before. I reread the words, and felt the love Edward must have had for his Jordan. I wondered who she was, and I how I was related to her. The journal was dated 1893.

I have been hard hearted and frozen inside for so many years, and you made me feel things I didn't know were possible. I'm sorry for the heartache he caused you, but it will be my eternal blessing that Andrew's unfaithfulness caused you to end your engagement. Part of me wants to kill him, part of me wants to thank him a hundred times over.

I looked around to see where I was, what time, what era. How was this possible? I was afraid to read more.

Your joy is infectious. I would do anything to see the wonder on your face like you had as we walked from room to room today in our new home. And you were so determined when you decided the house should be painted yellow so it would always feel like sunshine. You even insisted you wanted the greens of nature for the trim. I love your vision, I love your heart, and I will make sure you will be pleased.

"*Brandan!*" I flew down two flights of stairs.

Stepping out of the kitchen, he saw my face. "What is it?" he said softly.

"Are you in the middle of something? Have you got a minute?"

"Of course. I'm not doing anything that can't wait."

We got to Willow Tree and I closed the door. "I'm a pretty private person. I don't share personal things with most people. I wouldn't be sharing this now if it weren't important."

"I understand. Go on."

I told him about Andrew. I told him about seeing him with someone else. I told him about breaking my engagement and leaving New York in a hurry. He took a step toward me, I took a step back. "I'm not telling you this for sympathy. I'm telling you this because you need to know. Not because of us," I said, pointing between us, "but because of what I found. I thought about keeping it to myself for fear I was losing my mind, but I need you for balance. I'm glad you're here."

"I'm glad you remembered."

"I am too, because this is pretty unbelievable."

I opened to the page. "Read, please."

I could see the moment of awareness, the same reaction I'd had. He shut the book. The grin grew slowly on his face. "I guess that means the color of the house is gonna be yellow?"

We both laughed. "Thank you for that. That's exactly what I needed. But, seriously, is there a logical explanation for this?"

"Does there have to be?"

"That hadn't occurred to me. I guess not."

"Your life is defined by facts and contracts and sleight of hand. You're not in that world right now," he said, touching my cheek. "Of course this isn't typical, but I'm looking forward to it."

"I'm sure it won't be my last surprise, but that was enough for today."

"I'm sure it won't be. Why don't I take the strongbox and see if I can get it open? Better yet, let me get my tools. I don't know about you, but I feel like we need to leave these things up here. I don't want to risk anyone else seeing them."

"I'll be right here," I said.

The hand-carved wooden box was about eighteen inches long, a foot wide, and about a foot deep. I lifted the lid and was flooded with emotion when I saw the box was full of photographs—old photographs. Some were on cardboard, some paper, and even a few were what appeared to be daguerreotypes. I sat with my back to the window to get the most of the sunlight, preparing myself for what I'd find.

Faded but still in superb condition, I removed the first photograph from the stack. Astonishment flooded me. There in the 'cabinet card' photo was Brandan, at least a century ago—jeans, boots, a white shirt, and an identical grin. Turning the photo over, the inscription read, *Edward, the day before our wedding, February 11, 1893.*

"I swear I'm gonna stop leaving if you keep doing this. What is it *now?*" Brandan asked, closing the door.

I was frozen in time. "What is it?"

"Did you ever think *we* were the ones who were supposed to be doing this? That somehow something is coming full circle?"

"I can try to wrap my brain around that."

I handed him the first photograph. "This is just the first one." I said as recognition dawned on his attractive face. Just as I had done, I saw his shock as he turned the picture over.

"Has it occurred to you from seeing this that we might somehow be related?" he asked quietly.

"God forbid. Bite your tongue." I choked on the thought. "Before this is over, we'll know what it means. I'm on the trail now and won't let it go until I've found everything it's possible to find."

"I hope I'm wrong," he said with his lopsided grin. "I'd hate to think I might be this attracted to a cousin."

"Ah, Mr. Sweet Talker himself, but don't, please. I'm about as full of self-doubt as I've been in my life, and I'm not yet up to facing my demons. Doing this will take my mind off my own issues and maybe, just maybe, by the time we're done, I'll have regained some self-confidence. Are you still game?"

"Do you think you can say something that's gonna make me go away? I'm not leaving, get used to it."

"Then let's prepare for more shock and awe."

CHAPTER 10

Looking through the photos, my body reacted as though it had shifted into high gear. Many pictures were unmarked, some with names I hoped to recognize in the future. Lifting the lid of the strongbox, Brandan said, "Looks like this is gonna be your department, Counselor." Carefully he removed the top paper. It appeared to be a Deed for Edward's original purchase of the land on which Madeline Manor was built. "Each of these papers is going to be a discovery in and of itself."

"I've spent the last decade doing in-depth research. It's what I do best. I'll look at each of the pictures dozens of times, but I'll take my time with the paperwork – examining, studying, making inquiries – then I'll move on to the next one." Somewhat in awe, I said, "I see months of investigation in my future – census records, Social Security Death Index, state and county records, school books, online sites. I can hardly wait."

I set the box of photos aside. "Do you suppose Edward built the bookcase? And what would be so important it would require the intrigue that had to have gone into the design?"

"Nothing comes to my mind that would justify this kind of subterfuge," he said.

"I'm on overload," I said, standing up. "My brain's racing. How about we do a mindless task and open the quilts while I have you here to help me? Two of them are heavy and I'd like to see them. Would you mind?"

"Of course not." He put the strongbox aside. Opening the armoire, he lifted the first one from the shelf.

It was a Crazy Quilt with bright colors but a dark complexion. "What do you think of decorating with these? They obviously belong to this house. They're too fragile for the beds, but what about putting them in something like a shadow box on the walls?"

"I can build you whatever size frame you need to display them. We can support them on rods so no individual spot is strained. It will be up to you to decide where you want them, but they'll be transportable."

"Great idea!" I said as we refolded the first one. "What's the significance of the name Willow Tree?"

"One of the few things I remember about my Aunt Madeline is that she called me Willow. I never knew why. I always thought it was a secret between us and I loved it. And, crazy as it sounds, I love the idea of an elegant tree house, but I'm not clear on it yet."

"I've got some ideas. We'll do design elements."

"I don't mean to be a sap, but who could have imagined a week ago this would be my life today?"

"Do you miss him?"

His question surprised me. I gave it serious consideration, then gave him a puzzled look. "Does it make me a horrible human to say 'no'? I can't think of one time I've been sorry or upset or, quite frankly, even cared. I'll have to figure out what that means, but no, I don't. It makes me question myself and my judgment, so thanks for bringing that to my attention." I laughed.

He kept looking at me. "What, am I horrid?" I asked, hanging my head. "I'm not heartless, just surprised at how seeing him kiss someone else killed every feeling I thought I had. My initial anger has faded to total indifference."

Brandan put his arms around me. I didn't resist. "One day soon you'll face it, and then you're gonna be done. Cleansed, finished, over. And you'll get up, brush yourself off, and move on. And you won't have to hide from your thoughts."

"How do you know that?"

"A lot of times we avoid things until our brains can handle the truth. Hopefully there's healing on the other side."

"Sounds like you know what you're talking about?" I said, trying to pry.

"I do, but with a different venue." It was all he'd give up.

We opened the smaller, second quilt carefully. A classic Lincoln Log in masculine colors of brown, navy, emerald. "Can you see this on the wall in The Library? I plan on making it masculine in there – everything will be books and warm leather. It will be perfect," I said, running my hand reverently over the material. "I know I shouldn't touch it, but it doesn't look like it's been loved in decades. Do you realize this could be over a century old?"

"You have a lot of resources at your disposal. You'll find a lot of the answers."

"It's my strength. The more I find, the more I want to dig. I'm tenacious when trying to find answers— unless, of course, it's right under my nose, huh?"

"Don't ever blame yourself. You didn't do this. He's a jerk. The responsibility is his."

"How do you know that? What if I'd been more attentive? What if I hadn't insisted on spending the last month apart? What if I -"

"Stop it!" he said, taking me by the shoulders. "You didn't cause his character flaws. They existed long before you met him. Be thankful you found out beforehand and not a month later."

"Wouldn't that be awful? Even though my father insisted on a pre-nup, Andrew would still have been made a partner in . . . how could I have been so blind?"

"It didn't happen. You're not gonna marry him. It's done."

"I would never have forgiven myself if he'd become a partner in the firm my father spent his lifetime building."

"Don't go there," he said, taking my chin. "Do we need to get you out of here to clear your head?"

"No, it's okay. I'm fine, thank you. Sincerely, thank you."

The next quilt was about the same size as the first and was a Victorian Dresden pattern. Silks and velvets sewn to effect shadows and shimmers. It was beautiful, and the stitches were tiny, perfect. "We'll put this in the dining room?"

"It's good that we have these before we start. We'll be able to match the paint."

The last one was smaller than the rest. Folded lengthwise in thirds, I gasped as the last fold was released. It was a beautiful replica of Madeline Manor with all the colors it must have been originally. The yellow was still vibrant, the greens sharp, the fretwork delicate. "Look at the stitching in this, Brand. Just think of the time that went into creating it."

"Winters were long, neighbors were few and far between. They didn't have today's distractions."

"Even so, it's mind boggling."

"There was a survey done in the 1950s asking thousands of people how they thought their lives would be different when computers or robots could do things for them. The overwhelming response was, 'What are we gonna do with all of our free time?'"

"Yeah, right. Look how computers consume our lives," I said. "But the cold harsh truth is, I haven't missed it at all. I will have thousands of emails when I get online again, and maybe one or two of them will have importance. It's so much busy work."

"Do you want these back in the armoire?"

"Yeah, there's so much to do before we can even think about them. Who do you suppose put them away?"

"No telling. They look old, but it's not likely they were put here when they were made."

"Another one of those things we may or may not ever find out," I said, folding the smallest one first. As I bent the aged material, I felt something stiff just under the surface. Looking closer, the house appliqué appeared to be a cleverly disguised pocket. Goosebumps spreading, I removed a letter that was yellowed but still in exceptional condition.

"I'm not sure I can breathe. Will you read it?"

Gently removing it from the envelope and opening the folds, Brandan glanced at me. He read in a reverent tone.

Dearest Jordan: When I met you, I was a cynical man. I spent a lifetime in the company of dangerous and rough men, not trusting anyone. So I hope you don't find it strange that I am writing a letter to a child that isn't born yet. Keep this somewhere safe so she always knows how much her father loves her.

My darling daughter: I have not yet set eyes on your face, but you are always on my mind. It is a great responsibility to bring a child into this cruel world, but already I love you and will give you everything possible, especially all the love your mother and I share for you. Your mother is convinced you are a girl and has named you Willow from the day she first knew of your existence. You will be the best of both of us.

No matter what happens in your life, you must treat your mother right. If it is possible for her to love someone more than she loves me, it is you. Already she shares your movement with me so we can love you together. Already she sings to you. You will be cherished. You have the sweetest mother on earth. I love you with all my heart and soul. I want you to remember that every day of your life. Your loving Daddy

Brandan opened his arms and I stepped into them. We said nothing, each of us registering this piece of what we now knew of the past. When he finally spoke, his tone was low. "I'm pretty choked up too, but we haven't scratched the surface. Each new discovery will be a roller coaster down a different path, so let's not rush ahead."

"Wise words, and you're right, but wasn't that beautiful?" I said in hushed tones.

"And poignant. I hope it was Willow who packed it away, and that she treasured it."

"Who knew you were such a softie?" I said, poking him.

"How about I get you away from here and buy you dinner?"

"It's a deal. I haven't left the house much since I got here. Do you have something in mind?"

"The Pioneer Inn or the Amber Rose. Both are casual. If you haven't met Sam, it's time you did. He's the best of the best."

Sam was a hoot. Grizzled, wrinkled, not very tall, I estimated him to be about my father's age and easy to get along with. The Amber Rose was a charming diner with wooden booths, and a counter with wooden stools. It was welcoming, and I could spend hours with this wonderful man.

"It's a pleasure to have another beautiful lady movin' to town," he said with a grin.

"I won't be living here, so don't count on much, although I hope to return often. But I'll get Madeline Manor remodeled and functional before I head back to New York."

"Ain't that nice of you. Your aunt an' me was old friends. She woulda been mighty proud. It's a shame 'bout her accident, she just weren't ever the same again."

"I didn't know her much after that, but I have fond memories of her. She was a special lady."

"It'll be nice to have the old place shinin'. We get lotsa tourists up here and there's not many places for them to stay."

"We've got some great ideas. Brandan's been invaluable, and it'll be done before you know it."

"Ain't nobody better'n Jack an' Brandan an' Miles. You got yourself the best there is for what your doin'. You been up to the cemetery yet?"

"No! Where is it?"

"Your property backs to it. There's a bit of distance behind your place, but they buried Madeline up there."

"I had no idea. Thanks, Sam. And thanks for dinner," I said as an older woman came through the back door.

"This here's Mornin' Sun," Sam said with a grin.

"Nice to meet you, Morning Sun."

"Friends call me Sunni. You the one takin' over the old Stratton place?"

"That's me. Not sure if I'm braver than I look or crazier than I thought."

"I'm sure it's a little o' both," she said.

"Oh, and if either of you hear of anything, I have to get my rental car back soon. I need something simple to get around in. I have no need of one in Manhattan, but keep an eye out if you would. I won't need it for much and it'll just sit between visits."

"We'll ask around. And you got a good man there to help you. Not much he can't do," Sam said.

"I'm finding that out."

Brandan nodded as we said our good-byes.

"Would you mind stopping at the cemetery before the sun goes down? I have a queer fascination with them, and I'd like to pay my respects to my aunt. Sunset seems like the perfect time."

"This cemetery is especially interesting. I've spent many an hour there."

"Thanks. And thanks for getting me out of the house and bringing me back to reality."

"Get you to reality and then take you to a cemetery. I'm just full of good times."

CHAPTER 11

The sun was setting, everything had an orange glow, and the whitecaps were breaking on the water in the distance. It was the perfect time of day to be here. Dozens of stories were told on captivating headstones. Brandan was a few rows away when I saw the large stone with the inscription *Edward James Stratton, Born August 12, 1856 , Died June 23, 1894.*

"*Oh, no!*"

"What is it?"

"Oh, Brand," I said, taking his hand, "*Look.* Edward didn't live much longer after he wrote in the journal. He was only thirty-eight. My heart breaks for his Jordan. Do you suppose we'll be able to find what happened to him? To her?"

"There's a lot of material left in the trunk. Let's hope so."

"Oooooooh, she's your girlfriend," a young voice said from behind us.

"Well, good evening, James Gabriel. What are you doing out so late?" I asked as I knelt to be eye level with him.

"I come up to visit my dad every now an' then. Is he your boyfriend?" he asked, nodding in Brandan's direction.

"He's a friend helping me find stuff about the house I'm living in."

"He made my Mama cry. I don't want him to make you cry too."

Brandan watched him closely. He knelt beside me. "I'm sorry I made your Mama cry. I know how hard it must've been for you when your dad died. He was a good friend of mine, and I wanted to help you and your Mama as much as I could. It made me cry, too, to lose your dad. But I never wanted to make her sad."

"She wanted you to be our new dad," he said with the guilelessness of a child.

"I know she did, James Gabriel, and I'll always be here to help you and your brother any way I can. If you ever need anything, you only have to ask. If it's possible for me to do, I will."

James Gabriel appeared to study Brandan's face. "You remember my dad?"

"Of course. We were friends when we were your age."

"Sometimes I forget what he looks like. It scares me when I forget. Will you tell me stories about him?"

"You bet I will, but right now we need to get you home. Your Mama will be worried sick about you."

"It's okay, I can get home myself," he said, running down the hill. As he got far enough away that we could see he was almost home, he turned and waved and called out, "Don't forget. You're gonna tell me stories!"

"I won't forget."

Brandan took my hand and walked slowly. "After Gabe left, I tried to help April as much as I could."

"You don't have to explain to me."

"I know I don't, but I want you to understand. Gabe was one of my best friends, April his pregnant wife who suffered a devastating loss. She was scared and alone and thought I was offering something different. I didn't want to hurt her again, but I didn't want her believing something that could never exist."

"That must've been difficult. I'm sorry for both of you. It couldn't have been easy."

"I was between a rock and a hard place." He sighed. "Want to see what we can find out about the other tragedy a hundred and twenty years ago? See if there's anything in the journal that'll give us clues?"

"Yeah. I have a thousand questions and we haven't even started."

CHAPTER 12

The back door opened. "Jordan, you all right?"
Brandan called out.

"Why wouldn't I be? What would possibly make you
think I was anything but perfectly fine?" Even in my
own ears, I sounded inebriated.

"What's the matter?" he said. "I got concerned when
I kept calling and you didn't answer. Wanted to drop
supplies off 'cause it's supposed to get cold tonight and
I didn't want to leave them in the truck."

"Sure, bring 'em in," I said, somewhat in a stupor.

We'd been working for weeks and the house was
progressing nicely. The journal gave new insight each
day, but often raised more questions than answers.

"Drove by and saw the candlelight. Wondered if you
found something in the papers. Why are you sitting on
the floor? Oh, Digger, are you crying? What
happened?"

"It's my wedding day," I said through tears. "Wanna
join me?" I held up the bottle of wine. "There's another
glass in the kitchen."

"Oh, Jordan, I'm sorry."

"I like it better when you call me Digger. That
belongs to just us, to this adventure we're on. And
what are you sorry for? That I had a narrow escape
from marrying a jerk? That I was too stupid to see
what was going on under my nose? That the man who
was professing to love me was just looking for a fast-

track to a partner position with my father's firm? What exactly are you sorry for?"

He looked at the bottle. "If you're gonna offer a guy a drink, there should at least be something left."

He came back with another bottle and glass and sat on the floor, shoulder to shoulder. "You been at this for a while?" he asked, leaning over to look me in the eye.

"Not long, but I'm done feeling sorry for myself now, you go right ahead." I was numb. I was enjoying my state of mind, but didn't want to regret it in the morning. "I had a close call, Brand."

"I know you did," he said, leaning back, drinking his wine. "Wanna talk about it?"

"No. Right now I want to think about something besides Andrew. Tell me about Brandan Tobias Webb. Tell me what makes him tick. Tell me about your family and what brought you here to this little town. Tell me what has you so afraid of commitment. You know, just talk to me. Tell me who you are."

"Ah, the old third degree. My mom was a nurse, dad an accountant. I had two brothers, both older. We lived in Longmont and I loved summers because it was always peaceful to come here and stay with my grandmother. What I remember of my dad is he was a bully."

"Was he abusive?"

"Certainly verbally with his kids. I think it might've been more physical with my mom, but I never wanted to ask, didn't want to have to kill him. Strange the protective instincts that go on in a kid's head, like James Gabriel trying to defend his Mama because I made her cry."

"Are your folks still alive?"

"Mom died three years ago."

"And your dad?"

"Are you drunk enough to hear this?"

"Are you kidding? With an intro like that, you think I'd let you get away with *not* telling me?"

"I'm probably not drunk enough to talk about it," he laughed. "It's not something I face often, but you and I are sharing a moment here. People know about it, obviously, but you'll be the first person I've told personally."

"Oh, I love being the first. Talk."

"Dad was a gambler with a temper. He had siphoned money from a client's account and was being investigated. He and mom argued all the time, but one day it got especially nasty. Mom came running in from the garage, and I went out to confront him."

"How old were you?"

"Nine. I was tall for my age and felt grown-up. I couldn't let my dad keep treating her that way. I told him so. He raised his hand to hit me, but I was determined not to flinch. I looked him in the eye and thought it was better for him to hit me rather than her."

I squeezed his hand as he rubbed mine with his thumb.

"Dad loved to tinker with cars. He was working on an old Camaro and his hands were greasy. I knew I was gonna have to wash his hand print off my face after he hit me so mom wouldn't know. He was furious, but lowered his arm and walked out of the garage and down the alley. It was the last time I ever saw him."

"*What*?! What happened?"

"We had no idea, he just disappeared. It rained that night, we thought for sure he'd come home because the weather was bad. He didn't show up. For days I thought he'd at least come back for his car. He loved that damn car, and even if he didn't love us, he never would have left it. Strange that a woman can hate a man so much but be so upset when he's gone. My young mind couldn't understand. She should have been happy he was gone. All of our lives were easier, but she pined for him. I felt the guilt of a young boy who had made his mother miserable."

"It wasn't *your* fault!"

"I know that now, but I didn't at the time. Almost a month later, my mom went to the mailbox and found his wedding ring. She cried for days at his cruelty in leaving us like that, him being investigated, her not making enough to support the family. She filed a missing person's report, but no one took it too seriously for a man in his situation to have disappeared. It wasn't a priority. All the while I thought he would still be there if I hadn't made him mad."

"Oh, Brand," I said, squeezing his hand even harder.

"In the late 80s, early 90s, the internet wasn't what it is now. She looked for him for years but found nothing. She believed he'd run off with another woman, taken a new identity. She was finally able to have him legally declared dead so she could collect his life insurance. Things changed then, she had a little money, life got easier, but she never stopped looking. Guilt ate at me like a cancer."

"There are so many things a child's mind doesn't comprehend."

"That's the truth. It affected all of us in different ways. My brothers were thirteen and sixteen, formative years. Made them hard. I hated him for doing this to our family. It was destructive to a lot of lives, and so selfish. Like suicide, there's nothing the people left behind can do to change it, only try to figure out what they should have done differently. She was a beautiful woman, but she wouldn't date, wouldn't let a man get close to her."

"Ah, that explains a lot." I teased.

"It probably does. All I heard during those years was if you let someone get close to you, they'll destroy you. I've grown up enough to know that was *her* particular poison, but I'd never met anyone I cared to stick around for, so it was easy to follow suit," he said, polishing off another glass.

"I can't even grasp what that must've been like."

"It wasn't anything like what shook our world five years ago when the police showed up at Mom's door. They were doing construction on a local bridge about two blocks from her house when they found skeletal remains they positively identified as my dad."

"Oh, my God!"

"Apparently he took shelter there from the rain the day he disappeared. He was wedged in a tight spot and they found him covered in years of debris."

"Then where did the wedding ring come from?"

"Ah, good question, Counselor. He probably died the day he disappeared. The police speculate someone found the body and took his wallet, which wasn't found on him, and left his ring in the mailbox at his address, maybe to let us know he'd been found. No way to be sure, but how could they have known how the family would react to something so cryptic, or what the circumstances of his disappearance had been?"

"That opens up so many avenues of thought."

"Tell me about it," he said. "Here's the main one—twenty years of your life have been based on a lie."

"What do you mean?" Sitting in total darkness with just the light from a flickering candle added to the story's mystery.

"Think about it. You live your life believing you're the cause of someone running away, that this bastard up and left because of you. You live trying to make up for the damage your young mind believes it's the cause of, and none of it's true. He was dead the whole time. Think of how different our lives would have been if we'd known the truth from the beginning."

"Nothing in me can wrap my brain around all the nuances of that. How did your mom react?"

"You would've thought it'd help, that it would bring closure and healing. It had the opposite effect. She sank into a deep depression. She blamed herself for believing the lie, was eaten up for not searching for him more, grieved for the death he must've suffered. Somehow she made him out to be a saint and she was the sinner. No amount of rationalizing could bring her out of the spiral she sank into. It was nuts."

"What happened to her?"

"She was never the same afterward. I did everything I knew to help her through this new development, but she gave up. The official cause of death was heart attack, but I think she just didn't want to live anymore."

"I'm so sorry."

"We all have our own stories. They're what make up our lives. Look at Edward and Jordan, so much promise, and look how they turned out."

I put my head on his shoulder as he pulled me closer. "They thought they had it all in front of them, didn't they? And they didn't have much time left."

He set his glass down and turned toward me, taking my face in his hands. "Every day we face things that can change our lives forever. Look at you and Andrew. You were on a fast track to marriage and hit a brick wall. Edward and his Jordan were so much in love and then he was dead."

"Your life was changed by a rain storm," I said. "It can happen in the blink of an eye."

CHAPTER 13

We were close enough to feel each other's breath, mine becoming heavier as his thumb caressed my lips. "'Client' be damned, I have a feeling the next minute or so is going to be that kind of moment. I'm well aware I'm crossing a line, but I don't think there's any turning back," he said in a whisper.

His lips were soft, but the heat traveling through my body was not consistent with his tenderness. My senses were on fire. How could he make me feel this way with just lips and a warm glide of his tongue? My body came alive in a thrilling way as he lowered me softly to the floor with a hand behind my head. He stretched out beside me, never breaking eye contact until his lips took mine again.

I ran my fingers through his beautiful hair. His gentleness was intoxicating, and I wanted more. I pulled his mouth harder against mine, wanting him closer, wanting . . . just wanting. His lips trailed down my neck and I moaned. "What are you doing to me?"

"I've wanted to do this for a while, but we need to slow down now," he said.

"You can't be serious?"

"I'm dead serious. If we're gonna proceed, you're gonna be stone cold sober. I've dreamt of you like this, wanted you soft and pliable beneath me more times than I can remember, but you're gonna be fully knowledgeable and conscious when we go further."

"There's not going to be a 'further' if you stop now." I was trying to tease, but it probably sounded more like begging.

"Oh, yes, Jordan, there's going to be a 'further.' We're past client/contractor/casual friend. There's something here I can't explain, but I know I've never been here before. When it happens, your judgment and vision will not be clouded. I want all of your senses knowing full well what they're walking into. I want you to know beyond a shadow of a doubt where you are and who you're with."

I laughed out loud and sat up. "You're kidding, right? Although I want to strangle you for stopping, be sure of one thing, mister. In the two years we were together, never once did Andrew make my body feel the way it has in the last ten minutes. Never once did I get lost in just the pure sensuality of what was happening. And I promise you, never once did I want to push him down and rip his clothes off. So don't you dare question that. I was fully conscious of where I was and who you are."

"I appreciate that insight, but I wasn't speaking of Andrew. I was talking about Edward."

"I don't understand?"

"I get the confusion it must cause to read hundred-year-old letters that are addressed to you—your name, your situations. But Edward died a long time ago, and I'm here now—warm, blood coursing through my veins, and it's you I want. I want to make sure we're on the same page."

"Since I've had one or two more glasses of wine than I should and my tongue is looser than normal, let's have this conversation right now. And stop looking at my lips like that or there's not a lot of talking that's gonna happen."

"I'll have to remember that if I ever want to shut you up."

I leaned against the wall and patted the floor next to me. We sat shoulder to shoulder in shadows; the candle was almost spent. "I'm not in love with Edward, there's no question. I'm enamored with the fact he loved his Jordan so much and was able to express it. While I'm reading, I often get lost in his love for her and hope he said those beautiful words to her and not just in his journal. Frankly, it's easy to blur the lines, but I know what's real. That's not a concern."

"I think it's a safe bet from the things we've found that he was verbal with her, if that puts your mind at ease," he said softly, matching the mood of the room.

"I would agree. Listen, it's never been part of me to share my feelings, but we've already ascertained I've had one too many and I've gone through a time warp. There's obviously been huge changes in my living environment, every single thing in my life is different today than it was this time last month."

"It would upset anyone's equilibrium."

"Alone in this big house, I've had plenty of time to think. It's been discouraging to realize I wasn't in love with Andrew either, and the funny thing is, it was Edward's letters that showed me that."

Brandan put his hand on mine. "Go on."

"I was so busy getting where I thought I wanted to be that I didn't have time to date. Andrew was convenient. You get caught up in the rat race of business and time slips away. You wake up one morning and you're thirty-two and the best thing that's happened to you in years is that your fiancé cheated on you."

"Inheriting a rundown Victorian in the middle of nowhere wasn't such a bad thing either."

"You're right," I said with a warm laugh. "But what you're sensing in my affection for Edward is how he felt about his Jordan. It's endearing. He loved her so much. He was a hard and rough man who found love and it changed him. I want what Edward and Jordan had . . . only I want more time."

I picked up the flickering candle as I stood. "Thank you for sharing the evening with me. Can't believe I just spilled my guts like that. You may be right, I may not be as sober as I thought I was. I assume you'll still come over in the morning?"

"Of course. I'll get the supplies into the kitchen." Taking my face in his hands, he said, "I loved tonight, Digger. I'm enchanted."

"I'm still angry with you," I said, twisting my mouth.

Smiling, he leaned over and kissed me enough to make me yearn for this. "No, you're not. We're good friends. You'll still be glad to see me in the morning."

"Keep telling yourself that, buddy," I said, trying to sound serious. "Now get out of here."

CHAPTER 14

When I saw him the next morning, I was surprised how the memory of last night took my breath away.

"I'm still mad at you," I said, not entirely kidding.

"If you keep looking at me like that, I'll try to make you angry more often."

"Ach!" I laughed as I walked from the room, surprised at my new awareness. I wasn't sure this was a good path for us, but I wasn't sure I minded either. Halfway up the stairs looking into the dining room, something registered. "You can fix anything, right?!"

"I think before I step into *that* one, we should have some qualifiers." He laughed.

"Do you have a big hammer?"

"You sober enough to find out?"

Teasing, I poked his chest and said, "I need a big hammer. Right now I don't care who it belongs to."

"Coming right up—so to speak. Let me get mine."

He handed me a large hammer. "If I'm wrong, you can fix the damage, right?"

"It all depends, but have at it."

I smashed the wall between the parlor and the dining room. As the hole got bigger, I became more and more enthusiastic. "Dare I ask what you're doing?" he said casually, leaning against the door jamb.

"*Look*, Brand! Look what's back here!"

He was beside me immediately, looking through the destroyed drywall. "Will you look at that?" he said, a smile spreading across his face. "Let me help." With that he took his hands and pulled, removing large chunks of sheet rock. "Well, I'll be . . ."

"I'm *so* excited!" With childlike enthusiasm, I tore at the wall with him.

Less than five minutes later we had the drywall off. Studs enclosed a magnificent opening of oak pocket doors that were beautifully intact. "Why would someone do this?" I asked, disbelievingly.

"It was common back in the seventies to lower ceilings and close off rooms for energy conservation. Just be thankful they left everything here. Even the trim moulding was left untouched. Isn't it impressive?"

I threw my arms around him in the sheer joy of living. "Will you help me get the two-by-fours down?"

"Let me grab my tools and we'll make short work of it."

He came back with two pry bars and showed me how to use one to remove the upright boards and the boards across the floor without doing damage. As I worked in the dining room, he worked on the opposite wall in the parlor. Within the hour we were done with both sides.

We stood looking at the beautiful destruction around us. "Glad you didn't start removing the wallpaper in here. You would have been disappointed to do all that work and then lose the wall. Are you crying?"

"How silly am I? My fiancé cheating on me doesn't make me cry, but finding a doorway that was enclosed heaven-only-knows how long ago can make me tear up."

We were powdered in drywall dust, and there was debris covering the room. "May I have this dance?"

"Excuse me?"

"I'd like to waltz through the doorway with you. Our own form of christening. How many times do you think Edward and Jordan got to walk through these doors together?"

He took me in his arms and hummed a haunting tune. "What's that?" I asked, leaning my head against his chest, sharing an affectionate interlude.

"A song my grandmother used to hum when I was a kid. I haven't thought of it in years."

Time stood still for that brief moment. I've always been self-sufficient, but I was glad I had Brandan to share this with, someone who understood the emotions and history and nuances of what was happening.

"What made you think of this doorway?" he asked quietly, still moving slowly with me in his arms.

"Something I read last night after you left. I must not have been coherent or it would have registered sooner. I was reminded of it as I went up the stairs and there was no doorway between the dining room and parlor. Come here."

I took him by the hand and led him halfway up the stairs. "Edward said his heart raced as he sat in the parlor and could see Jordan's reflection in the dining room mirror. If you look, there's no way he could have seen her in the dining room if there wasn't a doorway between them. As I walked up the stairs and thought of his long-ago words, it struck me something had to have been different."

"That's my Digger," he said, taking my face and kissing me ever so softly.

"Two things strike me when you kiss me," I said matter-of-factly, lowering my head.

"Yes," he said, making the word almost two syllables.

"For such a strong man, you're incredibly gentle, and for all of your gentleness, it stirs some pretty ungentle responses in me."

He lowered his head to kiss me again, but I put my hand on his chest. "We'll never get anything done if we start down this course," I said, heading down the stairs. "Tell me where to put this stuff and I'll start hauling."

"I may not have said this before, but I admire you," he said.

"Whatever for?"

"For coming to this obscure town and appearing as though you've been doing this forever. Because you're smart and savvy and just a little bit vulnerable. Because you're tenacious and diplomatic, and not too bad to look at. That'll do for starters."

I tried to think of a suitable response. When none came, I said, "I should have asked before, but do you have some work gloves? I'll be a lot more tenacious in getting this stuff outta here if I'm not worried about splinters."

We cleared the debris in a short time. "The design work and ordering are done, crews have been hired, and supplies are arriving daily. Work will begin in earnest Monday morning, so prepare yourself."

"I can hardly wait!"

"We're going to do it in stages, but I have a crew ready to come in and make short shrift of the remodel. We'll get the major construction out of the way, bathrooms, kitchen, basement, roof. They're prepared to work six-day weeks if that's what you want."

"That's terrific! How long do you think it'll take?"

"For the infrastructure, we should be done within a month. Then it will be—pardon the expression—lipstick on a pig."

"I haven't heard that in ages," I said, sweeping up small pieces of drywall and dust that were left on the floor.

"Tomorrow will be the last day in a long while you'll have total peace and quiet around here, so enjoy it while you can. There'll be enough men around, it'll remind you of ants on an anthill."

"I'll try to stay out of the way. It'll give me time to go through the journal and strongbox, do research, look online for decorating ideas and furniture. I'm using the pictures to get a feel for what it looked like. I want to replicate as much as possible. I'm actually looking forward to it. You'll be here, won't you?"

We stared at each other. "It'll be hard for you to get rid of me."

"Don't read too much into it, but I'm glad you've been here. It wouldn't have been the same without you."

He touched my cheek. "I know, Digger, I feel the same way. I'm glad we've been able to share it."

"Will you make sure everyone knows Willow Tree is off limits?"

"I'll work on it personally. *Oh*, I almost forgot," he said with a big smile, "I bought it for you this weekend. If you decide you don't want it, I assure you I'll keep it—happily. Come on."

He took me by the hand and led me to the front drive. "Your chariot awaits," he said as he extended his arm toward a candy-apple-red truck.

"It's mine?" I said, covering my mouth in disbelief.

"It is if you want it."

"A month ago I was New York lawyer wearing designer clothes, traveling in high-brow circles. Now I'm the owner of a Victorian house on ten acres in the middle of nowhere with a view of the water, and I'm driving a '57 Chevy pickup." I threw my arms around him. "It's absolutely perfect! Don't leave before I give you a check for it. I don't ever want there to be any question about the ownership of said truck." Turning to look at it again, I held out my hand.

"Hand over the keys, mister, we're going for a spin."

"It's a pretty cherry drive," he said as I hit the accelerator before his door was even closed.

"It's candy-apple red, not cherry," I teased. "Where did you find her?"

"Sam asked around at the Amber Rose. One of the locals used to haul hay in it. He doesn't have any more need for it, and he was willing to part with it for a song. There was some degree of guilt in not paying him more, but we were both happy, so it worked out. Sam says if you go back to New York and want to sell it, let him know. He'll take it off your hands. I told him to get in line."

"No way. I'm naming her Mac, and no matter where I am, she's mine."

"Okay, I give. Why Mac?"

"Macintosh apples, of course. Oh, Brandan, *thank you*," I said, pulling it around to the back of the Manor. I kissed him on the cheek and hopped out, delightfully happy. "Look at what happened today. We found a hidden pocket door, I got this terrific ride, and I got me a new best friend," I winked. "Life is good. Now get outta here before I show you how excited I am."

There was a pause as Brandan ran his fingers through his hair, not breaking eye contact. "Please . . . don't. I want what you appear to be offering, but you're not really offering it. Don't tease if you're not willing to take the next step."

"I get it. I'm sorry. It's a deal. Ball's in my court. For all the things said and unsaid, thank you from the bottom of my heart."

"My pleasure. I'm nearby if you need anything."

CHAPTER 15

I was tired but happy. It was a conscious thought as I washed away the grime and powder that were left on my hair and body after a successful day's work. I couldn't remember the last time I felt this way.

My mind was busy as I drifted off to sleep—where would Edward and Jordan have shared a room? What would Jeni think of the place? Would I be able to walk away from here and just come back for brief visits? Did I miss New York and my work there? And Brandan, what an alluring contradiction, but I didn't want to think about him. An attachment of that sort wasn't in the cards for me in the near future.

Wide awake at three a.m., I read the journal I now kept in the locked drawer beside my bed. What was there sent me straight to my laptop for research. I don't know how long I'd been at it when my phone dinged with a text.

Been awake for a while, saw your lights on up there. Everything okay?

GM B. Come up if you want. I'll put coffee on.

Ten minutes later the back door opened. "You okay?"

"Yep, wound up and wanted to share. Glad you were up."

"Don't get me started about being 'up' at this hour of the morning. What pushed your buttons?"

"*The Romance,*" I said.

"I can do that," he said with a grin.

"No, listen, it was *The Romance* you were humming yesterday!"

"That's it! How did you find *that* out?"

"You won't believe it. Get some coffee and I'll be right back. Oh, and if I haven't thanked you sufficiently, thank you for bringing the table and chairs. It's made things much easier to be able to sit here."

"They weren't being used, and you're welcome."

I came rushing back with Edward's journal. "Sometimes my heart aches with his love for her, and sometimes I can't bear the thought we might not find out what happens to them."

"That's not possible. You're my Digger. You'll find out."

I leaned over to kiss him on the forehead, but he turned his head and our lips met. "I'm not crowding you," he said as his hand caressed the back of my neck, "but I don't mind cashing in on the opportunity when it arises—and, trust me, it arises often," he grinned.

I'm not sure how long our lips were together, but I was mindful when it ended too soon.

"Now show me what you found."

I took a deep breath to clear my head and pulled the chair up next to him. "Look at this. After I found it, I got online and found a recording of it. Nothing should shock me anymore, but when I realized it's what you were humming, I figured I'd lost my mind."

"Of course you haven't. I'll tell you when you do, I promise."

Handing him the journal, he read Edward's passage out loud. *Every day I try to act nonchalant, not wanting anyone to understand how deeply I love you. You're the only one who will ever know, and if we have several lifetimes together, I will never be able to tell you or show you how much space you occupy in my heart, my mind, my body, my entire being. I have spent my life cold and uncaring—until the day you walked in and changed it.*

Everything I have done in this home is to show you, to some small degree, how much I love you. I wake in the morning after having you in my arms during the night, and I want you all over again.

I want to give you wings to follow your progressive ideas which are so refreshing. I often think I must be the luckiest man alive to be married to a woman who is smarter than any man I've known, but kind and gentle as well. You could have been with anyone, but you chose to be with me. I will spend my life thanking you.

I know how much you admire Amy Beach, and how you have fallen in love with The Romance *that she wrote. It was enchanting to dance with you in the parlor as the violinist played her haunting tune. Dancing with you is something I want to share until we are old and gray, with many grandchildren sitting at our feet.*

Brandan touched my face. "We'll find out together. We can't change what happened, but we can make sure we lay their souls to rest. As much as it's in my power, you have my word on that."

Leaning toward him with my elbows on my knees, we stared at each other. "You were never part of my plan, Brandan."

He looked around the room, then looked back at me. "None of this was part of your plan, was it? It certainly wasn't part of mine. But I know somehow we're where we're supposed to be."

He took me in a comforting embrace. "I'm not sure where that's coming from or what it means, but for now, I know you're stuck with me. I somehow know it's you and me who are supposed to solve this mystery, whatever the mystery is."

"I promise not to dig my heels in and fight whatever's going on. I'll do my best to find logical conclusions, but I'm willing to suspend reason for a while because there's no explanation I have that can explain much of this. So I accept what you're offering gladly."

"Things will be different starting tomorrow. There will be workers around, and you and I won't be able to enjoy the familiarity we've had the past few weeks, but I'm always here for you, no matter what. We're partners, of a sort, and we certainly share secrets, but for your sake, it will be best for you to stay out of the way as much as possible."

I offered him more coffee. "Unless you ask me to stay, I'm heading back." After a moment of silence, "I understand," he said, touching my cheek. "I hope I'm the first to know when you change your mind." I thought about changing my mind as he kissed me goodbye, but the time wasn't right, and I wasn't going to force the issue.

"Trust me, you'll know."

"Hungry? Brought you some o' Sam's cookin'," Brandan said, sticking his head in the door.

"Thank you! Not sure I've eaten anything of substance today, so your timing is perfect. *And* I've had some fascinating finds I can't wait to tell you about."

He leaned over and kissed me. "Okay, spill it, I'm listening."

"Edward kept receipts. I found a hand-written Bill of Sale for this house from Jeremiah Abrams, the architect who built it. It cost eighty-seven hundred dollars to build. The magnificent window in the main room is an original Tiffany, built by Mr. Tiffany himself. You can tell by the hash marks on some of the pieces, and each year they made a new color, so there are at least six or seven years worth of colors in our window.

"But here's what I found the most fascinating. The window alone cost ninety-eight hundred dollars, eleven hundred dollars more than the house itself! Can you believe it? I'm gonna have to take out some good insurance on the window. I keep looking at it. It's stunning."

"Unbelievable. I guess the padding of the quilts kept the air out of the chest all these years and preserved the paperwork. Have you found much that's damaged?"

"Not at all. I'm surprised how it's held up, although I'm exceedingly careful with each piece. I'll figure out a way to preserve everything now that it's in the air."

"Who better than you to be undertaking this?" he asked affectionately. "You were made for this."

"I must admit, years of training certainly gave me an advantage in knowing how to follow-up and track down information. I'm thoroughly enjoying it."

As September drew to a close and October turned in all of its gold and crimson glory, I was delighted with how quickly things were moving forward. Brandan had them take the piano for restoration. It would take two to six months, but the piece was ostentatious enough it would be a masterpiece when finished. The receipt was in the paperwork. An 1890 Conover Giraffe Piano, it was glorious mahogany with lavish burled wood inlay. An upright grand, it held a magic all its own, and would be a work of art.

"Hey, Jeni," I said as she picked up the phone.

"What are you up to? Ready to come home, sweetheart? I miss you so much."

"I think I *am* home."

"What are you saying? You're not thinking of staying in the middle of nowhere and not coming back to the City, are you?"

"That's what I'm thinking, at least for the short term. This is unlike anywhere I've ever been, and I've never been happier. I might not want to stay forever, but I'd like to make sure the B and B's in good working order before I leave it to someone else."

"Well, blow me over with a feather," she said, using an expression I'd heard her say dozens of times. "Will you do me a favor?"

"What's that?"

"Will you come back to New York before you make your decision? Get into the swing of things for a few days before you make it final?"

"I'm planning on that."

"Really?! When?!" she said with an exuberance I was used to.

"That's the reason I'm calling. I'm planning on coming out around the twenty-fifth of this month. I'll hire movers to clear out my storage unit. No sense paying for space when I have over five thousand square feet to fill up here."

"I'll take the week off and play with you! And, you'll be pleased to hear, I broke up with Jared the Jerk."

"Oh, Jeni, I know how hard that must've been, but I'm glad you finally did it. You need someone who's gonna treat you like the princess you are."

"So do you, sweetheart." I made a quick mental comparison between Andrew and Brandan, but there wasn't one, not only in the caliber of men, but in my reaction to them. I hadn't told Jeni about Brandan yet. I wasn't sure how to broach the subject. It would be difficult to explain to anyone the bond we shared.

"Listen, I have a proposition for you." I looked up to see one of the workmen standing there. Something about him made my skin crawl, and it wasn't the first time I'd sensed him lurking. I'd have to remember to mention it to Brandan.

"No, I won't move to the ends of the earth, even for you."

Refocusing on our conversation, I turned my back on him and said, "I'm not asking you that, but if I got you a ticket, would you fly back with me, spend a few days here, spend Halloween in this Victorian mansion, and help me get a little settled? This is kind of a scary decision and a huge change in my life."

"Yes, yes, YES! Not only have I missed you, but this girl is in need of a vacation. It's been way too long. Of course I'll come."

"I'll make arrangements today, then email you."

"It'll be so much fun."

We talked for a while longer as I paced the front porch. "See you soon. I love you."

Brandan stood looking at me as I hung up, and I knew he'd only heard my part of the conversation. "That was my best friend, Jeni."

"Thank you for telling me," he said quietly. "Just checking to make sure you're okay, see if you've found anything exciting. I'm heading back to crack my whip unless you need me for something?"

"No, I'm good, just tying up loose ends. Listen," I said, looking around to make sure no one would hear me, "I was looking through the pictures again. There's one of Willow when she's about ten, standing next to the piano. I can't wait to get back. Even in the faded black and white it was magnificent."

"Put it next to the Tiffany window and you'll have a million dollar wall," he said with a smile as he headed off around the building.

My next phone call was to Father's secretary to set up a luncheon appointment while I was in New York to drop the bombshell of my plans. From this distance, he didn't scare me.

The light filtered through the hazy window of Willow Tree. It came as no surprise when I curled up with Edward's journal that he spoke of the piano. It was hard to conceive being loved like that, and easy to get caught up in the romance of his feelings for her. I genuinely liked Edward and Jordan, and loved the way he loved her.

My bride is sincerely appreciative of everything I do for her. Her love makes me want to please her, but she was a spitfire today when her piano was delivered. I thought she might swoon from the excitement of her surprise, but she saw the receipt and tried to take me to task for spending so much money. The money is irrelevant, and the $700 was a pittance to see such joy on her face. A lifetime of listening to her play and sing for me and our children will make it worth every penny.

Oh, Edward, you didn't deserve what you got. I couldn't image the pain in store for Jordan. And I was thankful the piano had somehow not been lost to the house. I would make sure its music warmed these halls in the future.

CHAPTER 16

The energy was tangible as I walked through the kitchen. It was going to be uniquely beautiful. Brandan had made this room a priority, and it was almost finished. The floors were done, plumbing completed, cabinet bases were in, sink and appliances and countertops would be installed later in the week. The feel and the flow were exactly what I wanted.

I saw Brandan standing in the parlor doorway. "It looks fantastic," I said. "They're doing an impressive job, and your design is perfect. I couldn't be more pleased." We had adopted a professional relationship when the workmen were around, but our nights and mornings were spent in intimate conversation about the house, the journal, and paperwork.

"What do you need, Baker?" he said in a more forceful tone than I'd heard him use on any of the workmen before.

"Wanted to know if you want me to get the cabinet doors installed, boss," he said, looking at me. I looked away, but the guy gave me the creeps.

"Start on the opposite end from Mitch so he can get the water line run for the ice maker. If you can stay out of his way, go ahead."

"I'll talk with you later," I said. Baker was the man who'd been hanging around. I'd mention it to Brandan the next time we were alone, but something was troubling him and I didn't want to add to it right now. I'd not seen him on edge like this, but he'd tell me when everyone was gone. The turret room was my favorite haunt in the afternoons with cool breezes blowing through the open window. I was gathering plenty of information from the documents to pinpoint a history of transfers and lineage, but there was a missing link that prevented it from falling into place.

I sat under the window with childlike anticipation. Brandan offered several times to get furniture up here, but I wasn't ready. There was something intimate about sitting cozily on the floor with the sun shining on the century-old writing.

Edward, too, was troubled about something. *I'm not sure where the danger lies, but there is evil lurking today.* The hair on my arms stood up. *I am content that I have made you a master with your knife, and have confidence in your ability to defend yourself should the need arise. My fear comes in that someone may surprise you. They will be sorry if they mess with my little hellcat.*

I was instantly on guard as I knew too well the "coincidence" of many of Edward's writings. My knife was open on the floor next to me. I was fascinated that the original Jordan was also handy with her knife. It appears as though I came by it honestly. I'm not sure how long I'd been reading when I heard the door open. I was glad Brandan had broken away to visit. Anxious to find out what was troubling him, I was surprised more than scared when I saw Baker standing there.

"I'm sorry, you've taken a wrong turn. The turret is off limits," I said as pleasantly as possible, but would be sure to mention this indiscretion to Brandan immediately.

"I'm exactly where I planned." He stepped into the room and closed the door.

When it registered his motives were sinister, I set the journal down, secured the knife surreptitiously in my hand, and stood. "What are you doing here, Baker?"

"I saw the way you were looking at the boss. Everyone knows he's got a filly somewhere on the side and won't look at another woman. Figured you might need a real man to satisfy you since he's not gonna be interested."

"Get out of here—right now," I said, taking a step forward.

"Ah, I see you're interested." He took a step toward me.

"I'll tell you one more time, get out of here. Collect your last paycheck and don't ever step foot on my property again."

"You won't think that when you've gotten a load of me," he said, unzipping his jeans.

I tried to walk around him, hoping I could make it to the door without a major incident.

He was quick and strong as he grabbed me from behind, but he wasn't expecting the knife that pierced his thigh as he swung me to the ground.

"You BITCH!" He shrieked, looking at the blood rapidly staining his leg. "Why the hell did you do that?"

Holding his leg, he came to me as I was scrambling to get away. He raised his bloody hand and struck me hard across the face, knocking me back to my knees. I heard the pounding on the stairs just before Brandan and Miles burst through the door.

"She stabbed me! The bitch stabbed me!"

Baker was standing over me. Brandan grabbed him by the collar and flung him against the wall—hard. "Get him out of here, *now!*" he said to Miles as he crouched beside me. Reaching out but not quite touching me, he asked, "Where are you hurt?"

"I'm not, I'm fine, just shaken up a bit."

"You have blood all over you, sweetheart."

I touched my face where he'd hit me, then looked at the blood covering my hands. With a slow smile, I said, "It's his. It's his blood, not mine."

He sat down and took me in his arms. "Are you all right?" He was tender and comforting, I relaxed against him.

"Yes, Edward warned me."

He stilled from stroking my hair and chuckled. "You know I'm the only person alive you could say that to and not think you needed to be committed. What did he say?" He resumed the soothing motion of running his fingers through my hair.

"He said there was evil lurking, that he needed to warn me—I mean her—so she wasn't taken by surprise, and he was glad he had taught Jordan how to use her knife." We looked at each other with total understanding without understanding anything. "I got my knife out and set it on the ground beside me."

"Are you up to telling me what happened? We heard him yell and came running. The police will be here shortly and you'll have to tell them, but I want to hear it from you beforehand so I don't blow up in front of people."

I relaxed in his arms and recounted the story. "I tried to walk away, tried not to engage if I could avoid it. I was more angry than scared, but the thought crossed my mind I would have been a lot more vulnerable if I hadn't read Edward's warning. Now *that's* something to think about. But not now." I laughed. "Brandan?"

"Yes," he said in the two syllable way I loved.

"Baker said you have a filly somewhere and you aren't interested in other women."

Miles came in the room with two policemen. I recounted what happened, leaving out the part about the filly. "Do you need to go to the hospital?" one asked.

"No, the blood is his from when he hit me, but I'm fine, really."

Brandan addressed the officers. "Miles might have mentioned that he and I were downstairs discussing that we were going to cut Baker loose today. He's been stealing from the men and getting in trouble in town after work. We don't need guys like that on the crew."

Miles pulled Brandan aside and whispered in his ear. The angriest look crossed Brandan's face, and he turned back to the police. "We'll press charges in addition to whatever Ms. Whitman's charges will be."

"Thank you," they said. "We'll be in touch. Sure you don't need to go to the hospital, ma'am?"

"I'm sure, thank you."

Miles walked them down the stairs. Brandan said, "I'll kill him with my bare hands."

"What riled you up again?"

"He told the police you'd invited him up here. That you'd been coming on to him for days and he was taking you up on your offer when you went crazy and stabbed him." His teeth and fists were clenched.

"You know that's not true, don't you?" I asked quietly.

"*Of course* I know it's not true. My God, Jordan, you're in shock, but don't ever think that again," he said, wrapping me in his arms. "We try hard to get only the best guys. Sometimes we hire temporaries, but we check them out first. Baker's record was clean or he wouldn't have been here, but I haven't liked him from the beginning. That's one of the reasons I wanted you out of harm's way."

"Except for you and Miles, I've had minor interaction with any of them. I don't make eye contact, I'm polite but aloof, if I have to be seen I try to be as inconspicuous as possible."

"I've been proud of you. Most of these guys have been with us for years. I'd trust them with my life, but every now and then you get a jackass like Baker."

"He's given me the creeps a couple of times. Thank you."

"I'm sorry I didn't let him go yesterday, but we needed absolute proof, and we found it right before you came upstairs. Let's get you cleaned up. The guys are gonna know something's going on, so I'll calm the troops while you hop in the shower."

I laid my head on his shoulder and held on for just a minute. "Sometimes I'm overwhelmed with the care you take of me."

"I'm not the gentle soul you think I am. I would've killed him if he'd hurt you." His head was resting on the top of mine when I felt his chest rumble with laughter. "As awful as it was, I wish I'd been a fly on the wall to see his reaction when you stabbed him."

We were both laughing as we got to the bottom of the stairs. Miles took me in his arms. "I'm glad you're all right. Brandan and I were looking for the son-of-a-bitch when we heard him scream." A smile spread as he stepped back, "But remind me never to cross you. You're one feisty feline."

"Thanks, Miles." I was weary all of a sudden. "I'm gonna get cleaned up. Thank you both again."

"You gonna be okay by yourself?" Brandan asked. I heard Jack come in downstairs. He must've heard what happened. Callie would be up before long. I needed to get clean.

"Thanks for the offer, but yes," I said, heading to my bathroom.

CHAPTER 17

I showered, then filled the tub with hot water and soaked. Would the afternoon have turned out differently if I hadn't been prepared? Brandan knocked on the door. "You okay in there?"

"Yeah, if you haven't heard signs of life in ten minutes, come back."

I was drained. Lifting myself out of the water, I dried off slowly.

"You decent yet?" He opened the door a crack.

"Just wanted to make sure . . . Oh, God, now I have to kill him."

I looked at my reflection. I was going to have one heck of a shiner, and bruising was already showing on my swollen cheek. "Nice. Not sure there's enough make-up in town to cover what that's gonna look like tomorrow."

He turned me to look closely at my face. "Does it hurt?"

"No, just feels lopsided."

"That it is. Callie and Jack are downstairs. You up to seeing them?"

"Let me finish getting dressed. I'll be down in five."

"Do you need help?" he said. It amused me he kept a straight face when he asked.

"I think I got this one."

"Look at you!" Callie said as she hugged me. "You poor thing!" She was several inches taller than I, and there was something comforting about her understanding. So much so that I was mortified when I realized there were tears loosening their hold from my lashes.

"Don't cry." Putting her arm around my shoulder, she led me to the wrap-around porch. "The sun is going down and it's beautiful over the water. Let's sit here. How do you feel?" she asked, sitting on the step next to me.

"Right now, I'm more angry than anything."

"Will you consider staying with us for a day or two?"

"I have too much to do here, and I'm not gonna let some jerk make me afraid to be in my own house."

"How many times did I say *that*? Okay, I won't push you, but know we can be here in a heartbeat if you need us, and Brandan's even closer."

We talked for a while, then walked into the house arm in arm. "You coming home with us?" Jack asked.

"No, but thanks for the offer. I want to stay here and not let him make me afraid."

"Sounds like someone else I know," he said, putting his arm around Callie and kissing her on the forehead.

"We're just a stone's throw away, so no matter what time it is, don't hesitate to call if you need *anything*," Callie said, hugging me.

"I can't tell you how much I appreciate it, but I promise I'll be okay."

She looked between Brandan and me and got a small smile. "I'm sure you will be," she said as she led Jack out the door.

"I've got plans for tonight, so I'm gonna head on out if that's okay," Miles said. "Tomorrow's Friday. It'll be the biggest push of the remodel, then no one will be here over the weekend. We'll hide Jordan upstairs, but someone will be around to keep an eye on you."

"I'm fine, truly. Don't worry about me."

Miles hugged me as he was leaving. "Glad you're okay. Brandan and I would have ripped him from stem to stern if he'd done more damage."

Brandan gathered his things. I walked up behind him and put my arms around his waist. "I'm not sure how to ask, and I'm not trying to push the envelope, but do you think you could stay, either for a little while or for the night—in my room—with me?"

He ran his fingers into my hair. "I'll stay, but this is like too much alcohol. I'm aware of the rush of emotions you're going through, and I guarantee this is not going to be construed as you opening the door. I have enough self-control I can do that. I was going to sleep on the living room floor if I had to so you're not alone tonight."

"I appreciate it, I just can't bear the thought of you leaving. Maybe that makes me sound weak, but I want you here."

"I'm proud of what you did today. Nothing weak about you, just the after effects of trauma. It's pretty normal."

There was no embarrassment later as I stood in the bedroom in nothing but a tee shirt and panties. When he came out of the bathroom in his briefs and a tee shirt, it rather took my breath away. His legs and arms were muscular, and I was surprised I had never appreciated how beautifully formed he was. "From an objective standpoint, you're an amazing specimen."

"Thank you, Counselor. You're not too bad yourself."

"Yeah, I feel like a peach. One that's been dropped, kicked, and bruised . . . attractive indeed. Brandan!" I got closer to look at the scar on his left thigh. "May I touch it?"

"If you don't mind my reaction to your face being that close to my crotch and you running your hand up my thigh, be my guest."

We grinned at each other. "Thanks for the warning." I touched the rough yet fascinating flesh that was rippled and shiny. "What happened?"

"The accident that killed Gabe—I was one of the first responders."

"Oh, Brand." I crawled into bed and propped up pillows. "Tell me."

"Not much to tell," he said, getting in next to me. "Gabe got the boys out but didn't have the strength to get himself out. I jumped into the small opening in the ice and was able to dive down and push him up enough for them to pull him out. I understood immediately what happened to him as my body was numb and lethargic. Someone grabbed me by the collar and didn't quite have the strength to pull me out, so he pulled me in inches. Each pull ripped a little bit of my jeans and flesh, but I was too frozen to notice, and too frozen to bleed right away."

I laid the unbruised side of my face against his chest as I reached over to rub the intriguing welt. "Do you feel guilty?"

"For not saving him? I had survivor's guilt at first, but I did everything I could to get him out. His death wasn't my fault, so, no, I've been able to let go."

"That must've been doubly hard on April. You his best friend, alive, torn up, her ready to have a baby, him gone—tragic."

"I survived, he didn't, she was scared, she knew me well, and for a long while, she expected I would fill his shoes. Nothing in me could have ever felt that way about Gabe's wife."

He looked down at me and raised my face with a bent finger. "Hey, Digger?"

"Yeah?"

"Move your hand, please."

Realizing my arm had produced an enormous erection, I immediately put my hand under my cheek. "I'm sorry. That was totally unconscious. I'm sorry."

"You said that," he smiled. "No harm, no foul, now get some sleep," he turned off the light by the bed.

"Brandan?"

"Yes?" he said in two syllables.

"I'm glad you're here. I didn't want to be alone tonight. And I'm sore. Brandan?"

The now-familiar, "Yes?"

"What do you think would have happened if I hadn't read Edward's journal? I thought Baker was lost at first. It might've been too late when I realized what was happening. I would have had to get my knife out of my pocket. Brandan?"

I felt his chest rumble underneath me. "I'm not gonna fall apart like a two dollar suitcase, but who's your filly?"

"There's no falling apart involved, Jordan, just the after effects from an adrenaline rush, that's all. And the soreness and babbling are normal, too," he said, squeezing me.

"Babbling? Am I babbling?"

"What would you call it?"

I thought for a moment, "Babbling. Are you avoiding my question? I'll go to sleep now."

I was asleep within seconds. My sleep was restless and fitful. At some point I was conscious of wondering how Brandan was able to sleep as my thrashing woke me several times. He'd just pull me close and hold me, and I'd fall right back to sleep.

"Don't come near me, Brandan will tear you limb from limb."

"Jordan, wake up, you're having a bad dream again."

"Every time I close my eyes I see him. Will you make it go away?"

He pulled me close. "I'm here. I'll tear anyone limb from limb who gets near you."

"That's funny. How did you know I was just thinking the same thing?" I ran my hand softly over his chest, wanting, needing, gentle, hard, until I was lower, caressing, pressing, squeezing.

He throbbed under my grasp and stilled me by taking my wrist. "Listen to me, love, this is all part of the after effects of what happened. Horniness is a classic sign. You survived danger, and what better way to reinforce that than to have wild sex? I won't have you this way."

"You don't need to have me, just let me have you," I said. I slid his pants off in one swift motion. "Please, let me do this. No reciprocity allowed, but I need to do this."

I was immediately between his legs, leaning over, my hair brushing his stomach, taking him in my mouth with no preliminaries. "I'm not gonna last long if you keep doing that." He gently put his hands on my head and tried to pull me up.

"No, I want you. I need this. Screw the adrenaline rush, it's you I need."

My tongue danced around his rim, and the sounds he was making turned me on more. I slid him between my teeth and cheek, and gentled as I rubbed my teeth against his sensitive head. "Dear God, what are you doing?"

"Telling you things I can't express in words. Just relax and enjoy."

I squeezed his shaft harder as I moved my hand up and down. His hands continued to caress my hair, and I knew he was close. "I want to taste you, Brand. I want to please you so much you can't contain yourself."

As I felt his orgasm begin, I realized it was me who was moaning, me who was writhing as much as he was. What a delectable experience.

CHAPTER 18

After a few moments, he pulled me up gently. I settled again in my secure spot in the crook of his arm. "You're an incredible woman—and that's one amazing talent."

His words brought me an inordinate amount of pleasure as his hand traveled to my breast. He leaned over and ran his tongue over my hardening nipple, but I stopped him. "No, I don't need that tonight. I just needed you. Thank you for allowing me to do that, but I'm quite satisfied."

In the dark of the night with just the moonglow illuminating us, we stared at each other. "Yes, I'm serious." I touched his face. "You gave me everything I needed."

"But I want to taste you the same way, make you feel the same pleasure." We continued to stare, him running a thumb gently across my nipple.

"I'm exhausted, Brandan, and wonderfully satisfied. Can we not go further tonight?"

He ran his tongue over my lips. "You drive me wild, woman. I'm not sure what you're doing, but you're an unusual specimen. Your pleasure is a turn-on for me, so I want you with the same intensity. But of course I'll wait." He continued to kiss my lips gently.

"Thank you, that was . . . that was . . . the best," he whispered.

Content, I curled up against him and fell into a deep, untroubled sleep.

When I awoke in the morning, my head was on his chest and he was running his fingers through my hair, staring at me. "Good morning," I said, breaking eye contact.

He lifted my chin and kissed me. "I don't want to go backwards, Digger. Last night was incredible. Being with you added a new dimension to this journey. Can you tell me about it?"

"About what?"

"I don't know. I sensed something I can't put my finger on. Like there's something wrong but there's not."

"Maybe what you're sensing is that I need to tell you I'm going to New York next week."

Stony silence. He sat up cross-legged on the bed. "Why didn't you tell me before?"

"Because I was confused about what I was doing. Did I want to hire somebody to run the place? Did I want to give up everything I've ever known to live here? Was I ready to leave my career? Was I ready to leave you?" Our eyes locked at that. "Was there anything of substance to stay for?"

He stood up abruptly and pulled on his jeans, shouting. "Anything of substance to stay for? Are you kidding? What do you think we've been doing for the past seven weeks, playing tiddly-winks?"

"Wait a minute, mister. All I've heard about you is that you're not in it for the long haul, that as soon as someone falls for you, you're gone. And God forbid they should fall in love with you because all they'd see of you is your smoke."

He was noticeably angry. "Was what we had not building a foundation? Did you think I was playing games with you every time I told you I wouldn't leave you? How could you do this without talking to me about it?"

We stood facing each other, each of us processing the emotionally charged moment. Softly I asked, "Who's your filly, Brandan?"

"Who do you *think*, Jordan? What kind of a question is *that*? Can you honestly believe that in all the time you and I spend together there could possibly be someone else in my life? You've never struck me as dumb, but could you not see what was right under your nose? Obviously, even my crew could."

"Obviously not." I'm not sure how long we stared at each other, but soon he was wrapping me in his arms.

"I don't want you to go. We haven't had enough time. Can you honestly leave Edward like this?"

"I might be able to leave Edward," I said, looking up at him, "but I knew I wasn't ready to leave you. That's why I'm going back to clear out my storage unit, and why I bought a round-trip ticket. I wasn't sure how to tell you all this for fear you'd think I expected something from you, and then you'd be gone."

"I feel like shaking you 'til your teeth rattle." He grabbed my hair and starting to kiss me hard. "I'm sorry, the last thing you need is me being rough. Honest to God, you're coming back?"

"Honest to God, I'm coming back. And I'm bringing my best New York friend, Jeni. She just broke up with her boyfriend, her grandmother has dementia and she helps her mom take care of her sometimes, and I told her she could spend a week here with me in the outer limits. She loves Halloween, so what better place to spend it than an 1890s haunted Victorian house?"

"You told her about Edward?" He seemed surprised.

"No. Frankly, I haven't told her about you either. You're gonna be hard to hide," I said, poking him, "but I want to keep Edward our secret."

He kissed my head and said, "I think that's best. Somehow it seems to be about you and me, and I don't want to detract from it by getting others involved."

"That's what I decided."

"Hello? Anybody home?" Miles shouted from downstairs.

I called out. "I'll be down in a minute. Make yourself some coffee."

"Crap, Brand, what are we going to do? He'll have seen your car."

"I'm here most mornings before anyone else. We're going to act like adults and not worry about what Miles thinks."

"Then I won't bother getting dressed," I said, heading toward the door.

"Get back here! What are you doing?"

"Not worrying about what Miles thinks."

We burst into laughter as I slipped into jeans.

"Good morning, Miles, you're here early."

"Wanted to check and make sure you're doing okay, but it looks like Brandan beat me to it."

Giving him an affection hug, I said, "You guys are the best. There were some ups and downs, but I seem to be much better this morning."

"Glad to hear it. Oh, look at you. I better not lay eyes on that son-of-a-bitch again. He'll wish he'd never been born."

"Stand in line," Brandan said, coming in the room.

"I didn't get a chance to look. Is it bad?"

Brandan and Miles looked at each other. "Avoiding a mirror might be your best option," Miles said, kissing my head. "Doesn't it hurt?"

I put my hand to my face and was surprised how warm and swollen it was. "Not unless I touch it. Let's have some coffee before the day starts and see what's on the agenda over the next week. I'm leaving for New York next Thursday, but I'll be back the following Tuesday. Oh, God, do you think this will be gone by then? My father will never let me come back."

"We'll keep it iced and the swelling will be down," Brandan said. "The color should be faded by then, so you should be able to camouflage what's left with make-up."

Work had been cranking along at break-neck speeds. "By the time you get back," Brandan said, "we'll have the painting and floors done, so let's make sure we're in agreement on each room. And I want a vision for what you're thinking of in Willow Tree."

"I'm not going to be out and about too much in the next few days, so I shouldn't be hard to find. I'm available when you are."

Miles took his cup to the back of the room where the make-shift sink was set up. "Guys will be here shortly and the kitchen will transform. You'll have a functional kitchen by tonight. The roofers are coming in the morning. I'll be around all day, come find me if you need me. Or if you don't want to walk through the kitchen," he winked, "just text me. I'll find you."

"You're good to me, Miles. In this short time you guys have become family. Thank you, you're a gem."

I was making the bed in my temporary bedroom when I noticed Brandan. He pulled me to him as I came around the bed. "Can't believe I'm already dreading you being gone. Does this mean I have to start reading the journal myself?"

"Only if you want to." I touched his cheek. "I probably should be coy and not mention I feel the same way. I can't wait to go so I can get back, and a lot of that has to do with you. But for me it's two-fold. I'm dreading clearing my storage space, figuring out what to keep, what to give away, arranging the movers, having to resign and explaining that to my father, possibly running into Andrew."

"He's not still working there, is he?" Brandan asked with some surprise.

"Yep. That part doesn't bother me. He was competent, and he was doing a good job with my clients. My father and I talked about it, and whatever father decides to do, Andrew won't be on a partner-track in the next year, which he would have been as my husband. Now he has to do it the old-fashioned way, work for it."

"Just hearing you say the word 'husband' associated with him makes me all kinds of crazy. I have to agree with Edward, I'm glad things didn't work out with Andrew."

He kissed me and I wondered again how such gentleness could produce such a strong reaction. When I finished making the bed, he was staring at me. "What is it?" I asked.

"You tell me. There's something I can't put my finger on. Something not quite right, something here I need to know that I don't. Any idea what that is?"

I looked down. "Maybe I'm self-conscious because of my face?"

"No, it's not that, but I think *you* know what it is. I'll be patient. I like to believe I have all the time in the world, but then so did Edward, so I may not be as patient as I usually am. If you have nothing else pressing right this minute, let's talk about what you want done upstairs. Now's a good time before everyone shows up."

CHAPTER 19

The next half hour was a pleasant sharing of ideas. As the workmen showed up, Brandan said, "You'll be surprised what happens today. You've seen small pieces fitting together, then all of a sudden you look and the whole puzzle is finished. That's what today will be."

"I'm gonna go hang out with Edward."

"As long as you don't forget which one of us is flesh and blood, I'm good with that."

I was lost in tracing lineage several hours later when Brandan kissed me on the neck. "You hungry?"

"Didn't we just have breakfast?" I asked. "I've gone back three generations so far to what must be Edward and Jordan's grandchildren. Want to see?"

"Let's wait 'til everyone's gone, then we'll sit quietly and you can tell me. I brought you food. How're you feeling?"

"I have no idea." I laughed. "I haven't been conscious of where I am since the last time I saw you." I stood and stretched as tall as I could. "I should set a timer to bring me back to reality every now and then."

While my arms were in the air, Brandan pulled me close, squeezing comfortably, relaxing some of my muscles. "I'd like you to stay up here 'til everyone leaves. I want it to be just you and me when you see the kitchen."

"I love the romance in your soul. I have everything I need right here."

When he stopped whatever that special thing was he did with his mouth, I put my forehead on his chest. "How can such a gentle attack produce such an extreme response?"

"If you knew what you do to me . . ."

"I don't know where this is going, but I wouldn't have wanted to make this journey without you."

By the end of the day, I was on my bed leaning against the wall with my laptop, getting tired. I'd traced the family history back to Willow and her husband Walter Ray. "You ready?" Brandan said from the doorway.

"It's ready?" I said, gleefully jumping from the bed.

"There are things that still need to be done, but it's usable and I think you're gonna be pleased," he said, offering me his hand.

At the bottom of the stairs, he turned. "Close your eyes."

I let him lead me into the kitchen. Moving behind me, he put his arms around me, hands on my chest, and whispered. "Okay, you can open them now."

In a dreamlike moment, the changes that had taken place in a few hours were extraordinary. "That's what I wanted to feel, the acceleration of your heart," he said. "What do you think?"

"It's spectacular. It's not even the same room! You're a genius!"

"I had a little help."

The room was warm and inviting, state-of-the art and efficient. Lots of lighting highlighted mahogany cabinets. I ran my hand over the granite. I opened and closed the refrigerator doors. I looked inside both ovens and turned on all six burners. The cupboards and drawers were silent, and the knobs and handles added elegance. There was seating around the island, and the pantry had a glass door.

He was leaning against the counter with a satisfied grin. I put my arms around his neck. The kiss was immediate and passionate. I felt drugged and moaned ever so slightly. Setting me on the counter, we spent minutes exploring each other's taste.

"I'll take this kinda thanks from you any day," he said, leaning his head against mine.

"Everything about what's going on is perfect. I've got this crazy notion we're righting some wrong with this restoration."

"I understand that. What did you find out today in your time travels?"

"I made it to my great-grandmother. Wanna see?"

"Yeah, but let's look at the rooms on the way. The bathrooms are almost done. It's coming together nicely. After the roof's finished, it's just spit and polish. That'll take two days, so we're close on the big stuff."

Turning out the light, I said, "On one hand you've made this simple. Your knowledge and involvement made this possible. On the other hand, the rest of it— well, it's not *complicated*, per se, but there are intersecting aspects. Your job here, our relationship, our relationship on an ancestral scale," I laughed. "Our finding the room and the journal and the name associations and the legal documents and the coincidences, I don't dwell on it because there's so much to take in."

He touched my cheek. "Does your face hurt?"

"Honestly, it doesn't. It looks a lot worse than it feels." We were at the bottom of the stairs when I smiled. "Race you?" I was halfway up the stairs before he even realized what I was doing. It was a good adrenaline release to spar with him like this, and even with him taking the stairs two at a time, I beat him.

"One of these days I'm gonna whip you," he said, laughing as we stood in the doorway panting.

"Beat me or whip me?"

"Yes," he said, stepping into the room. "What's your ultimate goal with the house?"

"Interesting question. I have a tie to it, although I don't understand exactly what that is yet, but I feel a need to take care of it. I don't expect it to be a big money maker, but it should support itself. I want it to be a refuge and safe haven, and whatever happened here before, I want it to be a tranquil place for people to gather, either alone or with friends or family. How's that for an answer?" I said as we got to the next room.

"Noble."

"I love this place. I love being in the mountains and the size of the town and being near the water and the people, and shockingly, I don't miss the crush of eight million strangers, go figure. It will be interesting after this to see how I react to New York."

"I won't be comfortable until you're back. A lot can happen."

"I don't get it. What happened to the guy that was gone in a cloud of smoke when someone said 'I love you'? We have something special, but I can't help but wonder if you're gonna be gone as soon as I let down my guard. What do you think, Brand?"

"I think I don't have a clue what's going on with me," he said as he kissed me. "What I do know is I have a desire to be with you, not just physically, but *with* you. I don't know what it means, but I know I don't want to lose it."

We had made it back to Willow Tree. There was an undeniable passion between us. I knew I'd never approached the intimacy of spirit with Andrew that Brandan and I shared, and it would hurt a lot more when he left than any betrayal by Andrew. "I'm not ready to lose it either, trust me. But for now," I said, putting my hand against his chest as he moved me closer to the bed, "why don't we go over what I found out in my journey to the past."

Kissing my neck, running his hand from my waist to circle my breast, he said, "Really? *That's* what you want to do right now?"

CHAPTER 20

"Don't you think it's the safest thing?" I laughed as I leaned against the headboard and pulled up my laptop, patting the bed beside me. "I found some confusing things I'm anxious to pursue."

He bounced on the bed beside me. "Does that include me?"

I went to the computer program where everything was saved. The playfulness that came over him warmed my heart. "It could. But look at this. I got back to my great grandmother. Problem is her name is Adelaine. Do you suppose Willow is a nickname?"

"What do you mean?" he said, nuzzling my neck.

"I thought my great-grandmother's name was Willow, but it says her real name was Adelaine."

"You'll figure it out, Digger," he said. He closed the laptop and set it aside.

"What are you doing?"

He hopped off the bed, turned out the light, and was immediately back. "I'm going to kiss you senseless," he said, again running his lips down the sensitive part of my neck. "You don't mind, do you?"

"Brand -," but my words were stopped with his sensuous lips. Whatever he was doing, I didn't want him to stop as his hand squeezed my sensitive breast. Even my toes felt the sensations that his tongue was creating. For only a moment I wondered if this was a good idea, then decided I didn't care.

I wanted this so much I ached . . . and yet I didn't. When his lips found my erect nipple I knew I wouldn't stop him. My hands wandered across his chest, I wanted to feel his warmth. He stopped my hand as I tried to undo his shirt. "This time it's my turn, Digger. This time it's you who's going to be blown away, so to speak," he said against my torso.

Was now the time to tell him? He would know soon enough, but this was too enticing to stop. As his tongue circled and pressed and pulled, his hand moved lower, covering me, moving back and forth, bringing moans that I realized were coming from me.

"Brandan?"

"Shhh. Just feel, enjoy."

He unzipped my pants and ran his hand gently into my soft folds. I enjoyed the slight noises he made that indicated he was pleased too. His finger entered me and he used the moistness to stimulate me, over and over.

"My tongue's going to be—right—here," he said in a husky voice. "I've wanted to spread your lips so many times and taste your wetness, feel you unravel for me, bring you such pleasure it will consume you."

I was hot, nothing in the world mattered except what he was doing. His finger was as wet as the tongue that moved smoothly over my lips. His words were an elixir. Whatever he wanted to do, I knew I wanted this intimacy with him. My hands reached immediately to unzip his pants, but he stilled them. "It's my turn, remember?" he said softly. "Do I need to restrain your hands?"

Something about his question sent luscious chills through me, and my deep moan made him chuckle. "Ah, my lady has spunk," he said, his lips caressing my thigh as he moved lower. His hand was again working magic, and I wanted his mouth there. "Do you have any idea what your moan does to me? Makes me want to nibble, thrust."

"Please," I said, running my hands through his thick hair, "please."

"Patience, we're in no hurry. I'm savoring you."

There was no other way to describe what he was doing than savoring. Softly at first, his tongue was gentle and carefully caressed me. His lips were still soft, but not as gentle as he moved his teeth over me and his finger was once again inside me. This was new, a feeling unlike any other, I wasn't sure exactly what he was doing or exactly what was happening, but I put my knees up to give him better access. I threaded my fingers through his hair while pulling his head harder against me. I didn't want this to stop, it was . . . it was . . .

My body clinched. The spasms spread through me in waves. "Brandan, please, oh, God."

His lips were tender on me until my body stilled, continuing with his soft ministrations. He kissed his way up my body with a satisfied expression . . . until he saw my face. "What's wrong? Did I hurt you?"

He pulled me into his arms, holding me against his chest, saying soothing words, then kissing my lips. "Talk to me. What's going on?"

I met his gaze. "I always thought it was me," I said. "I always thought it was because I was a cold fish that Andrew cheated on me. I've never . . . I've never . . ."

"You've never what?" he asked, kissing my nose.

"I wanted to tell you. I wanted to stop you so you wouldn't find out I couldn't . . . but I can."

"Are we talking about an orgasm here?" he asked.

When I nodded he said, "Have you never been with anyone but Andrew?"

"Yeah, I played around in college and law school a couple of times, but they were quick to be done, and I couldn't understand what all of the fuss was about. It was never exciting, so when I met Andrew and thought it was going to be forever, I just accepted it as who I was. When he told me I was unresponsive, I believed it was me."

"Unresponsive? What a fool he was. That's crazy."

"No, the crazy thing is I blamed myself for his cheating. Why wouldn't he want someone who was more exciting in bed? So as much as I hated him for what he did, I couldn't tell anyone it was my fault."

"Don't ever think that again," he said, almost angrily. "First off, it goes to character—honorable men don't cheat. Second, now you know it has nothing to do with you, it was his problem. And third, what a douche bag that he was so wrapped up in himself he wouldn't take the time to figure out your triggers."

"God, it didn't take long for *you* to figure them out. Wow, I'm still coming down," I said, breaking eye contact. "I think I understand a reason for all the fuss now."

Turning my face back toward him, he said solemnly, "We haven't begun to teach you the pleasures to be found between a man and a woman. We haven't even begun." His head lowered and spun me back into our extraordinary web. "But we're not going to finish tonight. I told you before, you're going to be damned sure before we actually cross that threshold that you know why you're here and who you're with."

"Let's put this discussion to rest," I said with some degree of irritation, sitting up, facing him. "I know exactly who I'm with. I know who you are and I have a pretty good idea after all this time what you are. I like what I see. I want more. We share an exceptional friendship."

"The closest I've known," he agreed.

"I've been so busy taking care of living I haven't had time for real relationships, even though I was getting married. In retrospect, it was all so businesslike. So know, without a doubt, I'm fully aware and open to taking this to the next level. Whatever that looks like, wherever that leads, I want you, and I'm ready."

"Then when the time's right, we will," he said, standing up and handing me my discarded clothes. When I was put back together, he pulled me in tight. "I hope you enjoyed that as much as I did. You're such an adrenaline rush."

"If I haven't sufficiently thanked you, let me express my heartfelt gratitude. Not only was it the best sexual experience of my life, it's going to be a paradigm shift to my psyche. I've always thought of myself as lacking, and you've given me this whole new freedom—incredible."

"Nothing lacking about you, woman. Not a damn thing. Again we're finding out that truth doesn't always mean what we think we know. I'll see you in the morning—early. The roofers are coming."

I walked him to the back door. "Wonder if I'll ever get used to the thrill of this gorgeous kitchen?"

"It's pretty spectacular, isn't it? People for miles around will be talking about Madeline Manor and its sexy-as-hell owner," he said, kissing me as he left.

So much had changed in the past seven weeks. I leaned against the door and looked at the kitchen, the transformation, and thought about how Brandan had made it all happen. And the thought of Brandan—he was not only one hot male, but unlike anyone I'd known. Real and deep and compassionate and funny and tender and clever and protective . . . and how the hell was he still single?

Turning out lights as I headed to my room, I considered how alone I was in this big house. I was used to being alone in New York, but with so many people pushing in on all sides, there was never time to be lonely. Already I missed Brandan. I was dreadfully infatuated.

Had something awakened me? I was restless and it was only four o'clock. I hadn't read Edward's journal in days, and as I pulled it from the drawer, I felt as though I was visiting an old friend.

Something sinister is brewing. I'll not tell Jordan about it just yet, but Simon Legree is being much too friendly for my comfort.

Simon Legree? Wasn't he the cruel and greedy slave owner from *Uncle Tom's Cabin?* Wasn't he the evil man who had Uncle Tom whipped to death because of his faith? Who could he be talking about?

He shows up all too often and I fear he has convinced my young bride he is not the evil man he truly is. I will not have him disrupting our lives, nor will I have Jordan believe anything but the truth. With her tender heart, I must be careful how I broach the subject so she doesn't think it to be jealousy. He's an insidious poison.

The meeting with Simon does not bode well for things to come. I fear he has an ulterior motive, and I must find a subtle way to warn Jordan. I hope he hasn't found my secret, especially since I haven't been able to protect us yet. I will take care of that soon, but hate to leave Jordan alone with him constantly coming around. Maybe I can take her with me on a shopping trip to Denver this week. She should enjoy that since she hasn't been feeling well.

Who could he possibly be talking about? Was this a warning in our lives or just a journal entry?

CHAPTER 21

Slipping into comfortable clothes and washing up, I looked at my cheek in the mirror. The swelling was down but the color was still intense. I hoped it would start to fade soon. Whatever would I tell my father?

When Brandan came in the back door, I was surprised how my breath caught. "A little sexual satisfaction puts a whole new light on the senses, doesn't it?" I said.

"My senses were already lit, but you could say that, yes. Did you sleep at all?" he asked, setting a bag of groceries on the counter, then turned to give me a brief yet arousing kiss.

"Yeah, I still got about six hours, so I'm fine. Got up and read a little in the journal. You can read while I fix you breakfast.

"What do you think this means?" I said, handing him the open journal. "And, I want you to know I'm so looking forward to cooking in here I could scream. I love to cook, and this is every dream come true. Thank you."

"Certainly my pleasure, especially if I'm going to be the recipient of your culinary skills. You and Callie will have to compare notes. It's always been a treat when she cooks for us."

"That's what Jack said. I want to have some signature breakfasts for the B and B," I said, setting coffee in front of him. "Maybe she and I can brainstorm and come up with basics."

"You planning on doing all the work yourself?" he asked.

"That's a great question, and the answer is 'no.' I want to oversee the running of it, be the face of it, make the decisions for it, but I want a live-in housekeeper in the basement apartment. There're gonna be times I want to travel, I'm not gonna want to do all the daily changing of the rooms, and I want the freedom to come and go as I please. I figure someone would like to live here free rent with a salary in exchange for cleaning and laundry. Obviously I want someone trustworthy, and it would help if they could cook. Any ideas?"

"A couple of them. I'll ask around. By the time you get back, I'll have two or three lined up that might fit the bill."

"Terrific. Now read so we can talk about it."

His smile indicated his amusement at my bossiness. "Wait a minute—Simon Legree? Wasn't he the slave owner in -"

"Yep," I said, turning the bacon. "What I want you to look at is whether or not you think this is an omen, or is it just Edward writing in his journal?"

When he'd read the page, I asked, "What do you suppose his secret was?"

"No telling, but I trust you'll find out. I don't feel like there was anything sinister regarding us in this passage. But let's talk present day for a few. Roofers will be here today. It'll take two days to finish both roofs, then you'll be leaving when, exactly?"

"I'm leaving Thursday. Friday I'll have lunch with my father, which I'm rather dreading. We'll fly back on Tuesday. Not too long."

"I'd be lying if I said I wanted you to go. I've got this irrational fear you'll get there and realize it's where you belong and won't want to come back to this remote town."

"Not gonna happen, Brand," I said. I put my hand over his and held his gaze. "If the time ever comes that I miss New York, we'll talk about it then. But I know what's there and I know what's here, and there's no contest. None. I'm happier than I ever remember. Don't get me wrong, I loved my life, but I want to follow this dream for a while. It may or may not work, we both know that. One day at a time, but staying there isn't an option right now."

The sound of the trucks could be heard coming up the hill. It was barely six a.m., and the noise of the dumpster was deafening. "I have to tell them where to set the roll-offs."

"Wait," I said, standing on tip toes to kiss him. "My new addiction," I said as he lowered his lips to mine. "Go on or we'll never get anything done."

Brandan came in as I was finishing cleaning. "Kitchen works like a dream," I said. "So much to think about, though. In addition to all the furniture, we need linens and dishes and glassware. That's what I'm working on today. I can do the shopping online and have it delivered here if you don't mind bringing it all into the house while I'm gone?"

"Of course not. Or you could just stay and be here yourself when it's delivered."

"Listen," I said, standing in front of him, "it's good I'm going. It's closure for me, *and* I get my favorite things out of storage, *and* get rid of the rest. Honestly, it's gonna be okay."

"I believe that, it's just that . . ."

"Mornin', you two," Miles said from the doorway. "Most of the crew's already here, so if you're up and about, I'll have them start unloading the bundles."

"Thanks, Miles, I'll be right there," Brandan said.

"I'm not worried, Digger. I'm not sure what this feeling is, but I'll get past it. Let's just say I'll be glad when you're back."

"You don't think it has to do with something in Edward's journal, do you?"

"No, it's not that at all. I think it's just plain ol' not wanting you to go. Not a feeling I'm used to. I'm usually anxious to see the door close behind them," he said honestly.

"It's not something I've experienced, either," I said, standing as close as I could without touching him. "I'm eager for it, and ready for the next phase."

"There's something about you going that brings out my protective instincts. I get that you're a big girl who's more than capable of taking care of herself, that you've been doing a good job for a long time. But things seem different somehow. Andrew and Edward and Madeline Manor and this thing that's going on with us . . . Just trying to figure out how to fit it all into neat little packages that don't exist."

"Edward said something similar last night." I grinned at the memory. "He was talking about how much he admired Jordan, and he knew what a good job she'd done to keep things going when her whole life changed, but he still felt protective of her and wanted to take whatever heartache he could from her. It was sweet. It's not necessarily a word I would associate with you, but you sure *can* be sometimes."

"Yeah, sweet, that's me. Just like candy. Wanna lick, little girl?"

"That may have been intended to be funny, but it didn't strike my body as humor. Do you suppose I'm going to be relentless now that I've had a taste of what it can be?"

He squeezed my hand. "Now *that's* a monster I wouldn't mind creating. Yes, ma'am, I could wrap myself around that axle a few times and not mind the spin."

CHAPTER 22

I grabbed a pad of paper and pen and looked behind every door and drawer in the kitchen, figuring out what I had and what I needed. I did the same with each of the rooms. It was my intention to get bare minimums now until everything was here from storage, and then fill in as needed. Thank goodness I had sold the co-op and had funds readily available. When we were done, I was planning on hiring Jeni to do marketing. Hopefully, Madeline Manor would start paying for itself soon.

The laundry was finished on the second floor, and there would be a small one in the Innkeepers quarters in the basement. Even the washers and dryers could be ordered online. Technology was remarkable, and I felt somewhat like a magician pushing buttons and knowing things would magically appear.

I had poured over pictures from the trunk for days. There were a couple of Jordan and Edward. It was uncanny how much he looked like Brandan, and it often made my heart hurt. I had seen enough of the photos to have a feel for what the original furniture looked like, and would reproduce it as much as possible. The house would be modern and useable, but I wanted the main areas to retain the feel it had when Edward built it for his Jordan.

"Having fun?" Brandan said from the doorway.

"Hey, of course. Who wouldn't have fun sitting at a desk spending thousands of dollars with the click of a mouse in the comfort of their bedroom? Who knew life could be so fulfilling?"

"I came to see how you're doing. And, just so you know, you've become the hero around here," he said.

"Me? What for?" I asked, surprised.

"Because you have single-handedly brought an influx of jobs into our little town. We've been able to put our locals to work, and that's a good thing. They're appreciative. We'd use them in Denver, but it's been nice to have some town labor for a change. You hungry?"

"What did you have in mind?"

"What I have in mind and what's possible right now are two different things," he said. "I'm thinking about the tip of my tongue just touching you, feeling you twitch, but that will have to wait for later. Ready for a break?"

"No, you didn't. You don't get to say things like that and expect me to be unaffected. You're sinful."

"Yeah, fun, isn't it? I thought you'd like to walk over to the Pioneer Inn, get out of here for a while, get some fresh air. Nothing more beautiful than fall in Colorado."

"I've noticed. But now I have to take a cold shower," I said, laughing. "Seriously, let me throw on a sweater and slap make up on this bruise and I'll be right with you."

"It's kinda dark inside and nobody in there hasn't heard what happened with Baker. You'll have a lot of defenders."

"Every time I think about what happened, a part of me feels like I should be swooning with upset. But when I start to feel guilty about what I did to him, I realize my guilt comes from the complete satisfaction in remembering what he looked like when I pierced him like the pig he is."

Blushing, I looked down, then raised my eyes to see how Brandan was going to respond to that. Staring at me with a blank expression, he suddenly burst into laughter. We laughed so hard my face hurt. "Good God, Digger, I'm gonna miss you," he said, suddenly serious. "I rather like having you around."

"You're not so bad yourself. Gimme a few, I'll be right back."

What started as a pleasant lunch became an afternoon of memories. We walked to the Pioneer Inn and had a rowdy, boisterous lunch with some of the locals and the long-time staff. Candice, our waitress, had been working there for over twenty-five years. She regaled us with funny stories, and worked hard at extracting information from me. While I wasn't about to fall for her tactics, the back-and-forth play was entertaining.

We strolled to the Amber Rose and spent time with Sam, who amused us with memories of people who had found their way through his establishment over the years. I could sit for hours listening to his stories. Being here really was like having an extended family, and it helped that many of them remembered my Aunt Madeline.

"You been over to the Carousel of Happiness yet?" Brandan asked as we headed back to the Manor.

"No, I haven't seen much of anything. What is it? Sounds intriguing."

"One of our locals was in Viet Nam. He dreamt of a carousel in the mountains to keep out the horrors of war. It's a great story how he acquired the mechanics of it. But the best part was he hand-carved over fifty pieces, thirty-five of them for riding, and it took him about twenty-six years. The whole community came together over it. I'll take you there soon. It's phenomenal."

"Maybe someday we could take James Gabriel."

"He'd love that. Speaking of which, do you mind stopping by April's on the way up? I have something for him, and I wouldn't mind the company when I take it."

"Chicken. But yes, I'll go with you."

James Gabriel was running down the hill toward us as we came around the corner.

"I saw you and Mama said it was okay for me to come say hi. What are you guys doing?"

"I brought you something," Brandan said, kneeling down and reaching into his shirt pocket.

"What's that?" He put his arm around Brandan's neck and looked at the picture.

"That's me and your dad when we were your age, learning how to skip rocks across the water. I'll be glad to teach you sometime if you want."

Tears sprang to his beautiful doe eyes. "Thanks for showin' me that. I look just like him, don't I?" he asked, handing back the picture.

"You sure do, and I brought it for you. Thought you'd like to have it."

"I can keep it?" he asked excitedly.

"It's yours. I'm glad you like it."

"*Like* it?! I LOVE it!" he said, running up the hill shouting, "Mama! Mama! Look what Brandan brought me!"

Walking home, I reflected on the man beside me—strong, intelligent, compassionate, passionate, somehow vulnerable, to say nothing of the fact he was sexy as hell. It would be easy to lose my heart to him. Poor Andrew, he was deficient in so many ways, and the more I was around Brandan, the more aware I was of Andrew's lack of depth.

"The guys are going to be working until sunset, if that's okay with you?"

"Sure, it's fine, didn't bother me in the least today."

"I'll come find you when they shut down for the night."

"I'll look forward to it," I said, staring at his lips.

"Don't you dare look at me like that." He drew closer. "That's an invitation if I ever saw one, and I'm more than ready to take you up on it. But we can be seen by every guy on the roof, and I'm not gonna expose you to that. Watch yourself, woman."

"Watching you is a lot more enjoyable, but okay. I still have a few rooms to order for, so I'll go finish. I'm not sure how long it'll take for a lot of it to be delivered, but I've been organized in keeping track of what I've ordered. I'll leave pictures so when it starts arriving you'll know where most of it goes."

"Not a problem." As we parted ways, he said, "Digger?"

"Yes, Brand?"

In a low tone he said, "If it makes you feel better, there's nothing I'd rather be doing than sharing lips with you."

He came in the back door as I was fixing dinner. "Last of the guys just left." He wrapped me in his arms and gave me a kiss that seemed a lifetime in coming.

The kiss deepened, and one of my hands threaded through his hair while the other ran over his torso. "I believe you may have unleashed something that'll be hard to put back in the box. Well, that's not exactly true," I teased. Coming up for air I asked, "Will you share my dinner with me? Relax with a glass of wine while I finish getting it ready?"

"I'll get the wine, you do what you're doing. How'd your day go?" he asked.

"Good. I'll finish the ordering tomorrow. I'm trying to track down some deeds. The names aren't making sense yet, and there seems to be a vital piece missing. But I packed them away until I get back. I was too tired and need to look at it with fresh eyes. Tomorrow I'm gonna be doing last minute things, then will leave early the next day."

He handed me wine and kissed the back of my neck. "I want to tell you something, Brand."

"Yes," he said in his endearing way.

"I'm ready. I want you. I knew it before, but what happened with James Gabriel today rooted in my heart. I just wanted you to know that whenever . . ."

"Shhhh, listen," he said, turning off the burner and setting the pan to the back of the stove. "We need to talk." He sat in a chair, and put me on his knee so my legs were between his. My heart raced as my stomach sank as I tried to anticipate what he could possibly want to say that could be so serious.

"It's not gonna happen tonight." I was hurt, I tried to get away. "No, no, listen to me. Hear my words." I wanted to cry, I wanted to hide. He looked at me questioningly. "We're on the same page here. I want you so much it hurts, literally." He laughed, then was serious again. "But not before you leave. I want you to go to New York, get your business done in a place that was your life just two short months ago, and see how you feel while you're there. See if you still want me, see if you still want to come home to me."

"Do I not get a say in this?"

"Of course you do, but not today. We'll enjoy each other tonight, but that's all. If I take you and something happens and you don't come back, I'm not sure what I'd do."

"I told you . . ."

"Hear me out. While you're gone, you're gonna have a lot of time to think. When you come back, you're gonna have Jeni staying in the house with you. When she's gone, if you still feel this way, there's nothing that will stop us."

"You're asking me to wait two weeks? Are you kidding?"

"I'm dead serious, and here's why." His hand was on my face and he was caressing my lips with his thumb. "When I finally sink inside you, when your eyes soften with longing and desire as I tease your velvet folds, when I watch your face as I penetrate deeper into you and I know all you can feel is me, then there will be no turning back. You'll belong to me, and you won't have any doubt about who I am and who we are."

"I don't . . ."

"I know you don't. I know what you think and I know you want me right now almost as much as I want you. I'm not gonna leave you unsatisfied before you go, but I'm giving you an out while you're there. I don't want to be the reason you make the decision that's facing you. And I couldn't stand it if I had you and you didn't come back."

CHAPTER 23

As the wheels set down on the tarmac at LaGuardia, scenes from the past thirty-six hours continued to roll through my heart. A multifaceted man, Brandan loved me to completion twice, and I could only dream about what complete fulfillment was going to be.

"For you, so much of it's in your mind," he had said against my lips. "I love that one of your greatest turn-ons is when I tell you what I'm going to do to you. A well-placed touch, some sexy words, and you're on fire. And that, in turn, arouses the hell out of me."

When we weren't physically loving each other, we were engrossed in the past, the present, the future. There's not much he can't do, and I finally let myself relax and understand I had fallen in love with him. He had been wise in his decision to hold off. Not only did it make me want him more, but he knew, even better than I, how much I had in front of me. I turned my attention to the coming week, to being back in the thick of Manhattan life, to explaining to my father why I wasn't coming back. He was going to be upset.

I hadn't allowed myself time to think of what ending this chapter of my life, no matter how temporarily, was going to mean, but I knew I was ready for it. Even if I wasn't there forever, I loved Colorado and the people in the town, and it gratified me to think about getting the B and B running. I was making the right decision for me for now.

Jeni threw her arms around me as I got out of the taxi in front of her co-op. "I'm so happy to see you! I left work at noon to get things ready. Let's get your luggage and get this party started."

"This is it," I said. "One nice outfit to meet my father tomorrow is all I needed. The rest is jeans and a few tops since we're gonna be doing dirty work for the next few days. Oh, honey, it's *so* good to see you. I've missed you."

"You sure you want to go through with this?" she asked as we climbed the stairs.

"No doubt about it. The next few days will be difficult, but I'll get through that and then I have a whole new world waiting for me."

"My, my, sounds like there might be a man involved. Let's get prettied up and go have dinner. You can tell me all about him."

We ate at one of our favorite restaurants. I told her about the house, the town, all about why I was making my decision, and how much I was dreading tomorrow. I didn't tell her about Edward. I'm not sure I would ever confide the strange happenings of my long-ago ancestor. He was our secret. Then I told her about Brandan. She was thrilled and had a dozen questions.

"So, is he any good?" was, of course, her first question.

"You're terrible."

"Ah, I can see by your blush he must be. We know Andrew was a dud, so now I can't wait to meet this hunk."

"Yeah, I'm looking forward to you meeting him too. I'm always conscious that not only am I happy, but he's as crazy about me as I am about him. Andrew and I were just . . . were just . . . there. But it was a classic case of not being able to see the forest for the trees.

Did you know he's still working at Whitman and Burke?"

"Yeah, I ran into him and some brunette the other day. It was all I could do not to spit on him. I'm the one that's the screw-up in relationships," she said, "and you've always had the right words for me when my world crashes. I wanted to give you back your own strength when things went wrong with Andrew, but my anger got in the way."

"Let go of it. Ending that relationship was such a good thing, no matter how it happened. I'm so thankful things turned out the way they did. I could be married to him and *then* find out about his cheating ways. And what I got is *so* much better than what I had. Dear Lord, wait til you meet Brandan. Just thinking of him makes my heart turn over."

I was exhausted as we walked the few blocks to her place. It was good to be with her. We sat with the lights out and two candles burning, finishing a glass of wine. "This has been lovely. It's easy to settle back into the familiar, but I don't want to be here anymore. I'll be curious to see what you think of Colorado."

"If you love it, I'm sure I will. But I still wish we could have found a different way to end your engagement, at least."

"Think about it, Jeni. It was done in an instant. There were no fights, no questioning whether I should stay or go, it was just over. And, with all of my tough exterior and the fact that I was spending hours a day reading contracts and doing research, I'm a closet romantic. I wanted the house and the babies and everything that went with it."

"You? Jordanna Olivia? A romantic? Well, blow me over with a feather."

"Yeah, I guess I can see how that would be hard to believe. It's easy to get caught up in the rat race of New York, and one morning you wake up and wonder what you've traded for your success. I wanted the dream Andrew was offering so much I didn't slow down long enough to question if he was supposed to be part of it. I'll be eternally grateful it ended when it did."

"That's the truth, isn't it? Some mornings I wake up and wonder what it's all for. We worked so hard to get where we are, but are we really living the dream? God, listen to us. Let's get to bed. You've got a long day ahead of you and I'm babbling."

"Not at all, and there's a whole new world out there. I've been intrigued finding different facets of it."

"Let's get the next few days out of the way and get the hell out of Dodge. I haven't had a vacation in over a year, and I'm more than ready for a break. You always told me what a creep Jared was, but I wouldn't listen. Why do you suppose I'm attracted to the ones who think they're the center of the known universe?"

"The ones who are emotionally unavailable and care only about themselves? You do seem to have a knack," I said affectionately. "Don't you think recognizing it is half the battle though?"

"Yes, oh wise one, let's hope so. Okay, so you meet your father for lunch tomorrow. When that trauma is over, we'll have a few to celebrate. Good so far?"

"Yep. We'll have plenty of free hours to visit old haunts. I feel like I'm saying good-bye to everything. I'll miss it, but not enough to stay."

Walking into the offices of Whitman and Burke the following morning, I held my head high and carried myself as though I owned the place. Well, technically I did since I was a partner in the firm, but I refused to be uncomfortable. There was a good possibility Andrew would be here and these people were still working with him. The last thing I wanted was for anyone to look at me with pity, or to even think I had lost something in our breakup. I was the victor, plain and simple.

My initial worry was for naught. I was greeted with handshakes and hugs from everyone I encountered, everyone thrilled I was back 'where I belonged' and 'how was your trip?' and 'where the heck is Nederland?' After fifteen or twenty minutes of friendly chatter, I saw Andrew standing in a doorway. You could have heard a pin drop as everyone waited to see how this first meeting would go. Knowing I was mentally healthy and in control, I walked forward, extended my hand, and said, loud enough for all to hear, "Andrew, so good to see you, I hope you're doing well."

The look of surprise that crossed his face was gratifying. Not the encounter he expected, I'm sure, when he came to the office that morning. "Jordan." He nodded his head and took my offered hand. "You back to work now?"

"Here to have lunch with Father. Good to see you," I said as I walked away. And the truth of it was, it *was* good to see him. Not an ache, not a sorrow, not anything but an overwhelming sense of relief I was not married to this blond Adonis.

Halfway down the corridor to Father's office, Andrew called out. "Jordan?"

Turning, I waited for him to reach me. "Can we talk for a moment? My office?"

Not wanting to give him the upper hand of familiarity, I said, "We can talk in one of the conference rooms." I was early and didn't mind sparing a few minutes to hear what he had to say.

Taking a seat across the table from each other, I could picture the buzz that was flying on the other side of the closed door. For a fleeting moment I was tempted to turn on the intercom to let them listen in, but having no idea the angle of the upcoming conversation, I let that brief but fun thought slip away.

"That was an incredibly childish and cruel thing for you to do," he said.

I'm not sure what I was expecting, but this wasn't it. "Excuse me?"

"Don't you think you could have at least talked to me about it before you almost single handedly ruined my career?"

At that point I decided silence would be the better part of valor. Everything in my being was screaming that I was thankful I had escaped this fate.

"When I was in law school, my father lost the family fortune," he said. I was surprised by that, but wondered why he was telling me now. I remained silent. "I had a lot of brains, but no longer had money. When I graduated from law school, I had a mound of debt, but knew I was going to be a stellar lawyer. I was smart enough to land a job here, one of the most prestigious firms in the City, and charming enough to land the boss's daughter, putting me on the fast track to partner."

I don't know whether or not my gasp was audible, but I was shaking in the face of his arrogance. My phone was silenced, but I saw a text message come in from Brandan. *Read some of the journal last night. Wanted to encourage you with Edward's words—'no one is stronger, no man or woman I have ever known, than my Jordan'—just thought you needed to hear that.*

What perfect timing. Andrew seemed surprised when a smile crossed my face. "What a wonderful sense of closure it's been to see you, Andrew. Take care of yourself," I said, walking to the door.

As I reached for the door knob, he said, "I never loved you, you know. Mary Ann and I have been together since college, but she has no financial stability. She understands, and doesn't expect monogamy."

Okay, that one hurt, but I'd be damned before I gave any indication the barb had found a mark. With head held high, I walked to my father's suite and thought

Edward was right. Jordan *is* an incredibly strong woman. Thank you for that, Brandan.

CHAPTER 24

My father was handing Carol a file at her desk when he saw me. In a rare display of affection, he wrapped me in his arms. I smelled years of memories and healed wounds from this tough and rigid man who loved his daughter as much as it was possible for him to care for anyone.

"Jordanna, I have sorely missed you. It's about time you came back where you belong."

"It's so good to see you, Father. Ready for lunch?"

After exchanging pleasantries with Carol, we headed down his private elevator to a waiting car. "Eleven Madison Park, Madden," he said to the driver as our silent ride pulled into blaring New York traffic.

"So how was your little adventure? Glad to be back in the City after roughing it for almost two months?"

"Hardly roughing it, Father. It was actually quite fulfilling."

"Well, I'm glad you're back. Andrew is good, but you've heard me say more than once, he doesn't hold a candle to my Jordanna."

I appreciated his words, but I wanted to wait until we were sitting in a crowded restaurant to tell him my news. He had too much pride to allow anyone around him to see he was upset, so my bombshell wouldn't be nearly as explosive with bystanders. Maybe I wasn't as strong as I thought.

"You'll have to get past the initial introduction again, but I know you're strong enough to be able to work together for the clients. If you decide you genuinely don't want to work with him, we'll reassign one or the other of you to different cases."

"I already saw him when I came in."

"Good, good, glad that's behind you." No solicitation for how it went, no assumption there could possibly have been anything wrong, just father, oblivious to the emotional entrapments of life. When I was alone, I would lick my wounds and relive Andrew's words, but for now I was Riley Whitman's daughter, and would comport myself as such as we entered this subdued restaurant that was filling with New York's elite.

"Good afternoon, Mr. Whitman, Ms. Whitman. This way, please," the host said as we were led through the hallowed confines to the magnificent, balcony-level private room that overlooks the main dining area and has spectacular views of Madison Square Park. I wondered how Brandan would have reacted to this place, and if he would have enjoyed it or thought it terribly pretentious.

Actually, it would be difficult for anyone not to think it was pretentious, but I loved it here. It was where father and I came when there were important conversations to be had. With almost a month-long wait for reservations, I had to hand it to Carol's efficiency that she knew right where we'd want to be and how to get us here.

Lunch was served and wine poured when father got down to business. "When are you planning on being back in the office? We'll get your workload reassigned. It will be nice to have you back. I've actually missed you around the office. Few have the common sense you do, and while I like Andrew, he just doesn't have your intuition."

"He doesn't have much of a soul or a moral compass either, but maybe that's what will make him a good lawyer," I said teasingly. "Listen, father, I need to tell you something."

"I don't like the sounds of this," he said with a frown, taking a bite of his succulent salmon.

"I love you and I love the opportunity I've had, but I'm taking a break and not coming back right now."

Only years of training and, I'm sure, an awareness of our surroundings, kept his voice even and his expression unchanged when he said, "What foolishness is this, Jordanna?"

"Oh, Father, I'm happier than I've been in my life. I want to give it a shot. I love the house, the place, the people, and for now, the lifestyle. I've had almost two months to think about it, and this is the best decision for me for my life right now."

"Does this have anything to do with Andrew?" he asked, looking me in the eye.

"Good heavens no, but thank you for asking. Breaking our engagement was not only one of the best things that's happened to me, but it was a close call I will be eternally grateful for avoiding. There's not much redeemable about him in my estimation, but he's a good lawyer and he can schmooze the clients well, so maybe he'll be an asset. You're the one that needs to figure that out. I've already spent more time thinking about him today than I want to for the rest of my life."

"Is it money? You know you only have to name your price and it's yours."

I was surprised at that. Placing my hand over his, I said, "Oh, Daddy, I wish I could explain to you how happy I am. I'm in a situation I never conceived of, and I feel like I've come home. I don't know what the future holds, but I'm ready for this phase."

"You haven't called me 'daddy' in twenty years. You *must* like it there. But I hope you're not making the biggest mistake of your life. You're in your prime. You've made a name for yourself and you've made me proud. I want you to be absolutely certain you're not throwing your life away. You've worked too hard to get where you're going to chuck it all for nothing."

"Thank you for understanding. If anything changes, I'll be back in a heartbeat," I said, somewhat manipulatively. "In the meantime, the B and B should be close to being finished over the next month, and I'd love for you and Mother to visit for Thanksgiving. Jeni will be there, and it's going to be a gathering of locals. I wish you'd think about it."

"We'll give it some thought. Sorry you missed your mother this trip, but I'm sure she's enjoying her shopping in Paris with her friends. The money that woman can spend."

"Don't I know it? She could help relieve the national debt with one of her jaunts. You've always been so patient with her."

"Don't have a lot of choice. She is who she is. I'll check with Carol and see if I can clear my calendar. Now tell me what has you all fired up about this hole in the wall."

Not only was I pleased with the camaraderie we shared, but along with letting go of the hurtful words thrown at me by Andrew earlier, I was determined to hold on to the first time in memory my father had told me he was proud of me. All in all, a good day indeed.

The next three days passed in a flurry of activity with the evenings spent visiting friends at favorite watering holes. I had moments of doubt when I thought about all I was giving up, but nothing was going to sway me. Just the thought of Brandan and Madeline Manor were enough to make me anxious to be back. Texts from Brandan were sweet and endearing and somehow vulnerable.

I'm not worried what you'll find there, but I'm looking forward to holding you in my arms again.

Edward's Jordan went to visit her cousin who had given birth to twins. Edward missed her a lot too.

*I'm conscious of how different your world is there,
but you fit in anywhere. This town needs you too.*

*Think you're going to be pleased with the progress.
Furniture and items showing up by the truckloads.*

*You and Jeni have your work cut out for you. Trying
to put boxes in rooms where they belong.*

*Living room furniture arrived today. I'm impressed.
You've hit just the right tone.*

And so it went. Gentle reminders that he was there,
that there was a life waiting for me that included
him—and a lot of work.

"Listen," I said as the moving truck left. "I know
this has been exhausting, and now I'm feeling like a
fraud asking you to come for a vacation that's not
gonna be a vacation at all."

"When have you ever known me be to be afraid of
hard work, Jordanna Olivia?" With a laugh she said, "I
always think of your father when I say that. So formal,
but it's a beautiful name for my beautiful friend.
What's on the agenda?"

"Most of the construction is finished. Before I left, I
ordered furnishings, bedding, dishes—you name it, I
ordered it. Brandan says a lot of it's been delivered in
the past two days, and they're trying to put it in the
appropriate place, but it's gonna be a nightmare of
unpacking. I guess what I'm trying to say is, if you
want to postpone your trip, you can. Or you can play in
Denver, but it may be alone. I just want you to know
what you're walking into."

"Are you kidding? Setting up house like that? Every
girl's dream come true, especially since it's on *your*
dime."

"What just left on the truck will go in the basement
apartment for the Innkeeper."

"We certainly won't be bored. Any thought to having
Halloween at your place?"

"I wanted to, but when we get home it'll only be two
days away, so I think it's out of the question this year.

They'll be doing something at one of the local places. I promise, you won't be disappointed. And I have some extraordinary outfits I found in a closet at the house that should fit us. We'll have so much fun. And I can't wait for you to meet Brandan. He makes my toes curl."

"Does he have a brother?" Jeni said suggestively. "Hell, no, forget I asked. I'm swearing off men. I seem to attract the creeps."

"You've just been looking under the wrong rocks. He's out there, we'll find him."

CHAPTER 25

Arriving in the airport terminal, Jeni said, "You weren't kidding," in a stage whisper after Brandan finished an embrace and kiss that left me weak in the knees. Touching my cheek, we said a thousand words in that glance. With an arm still around me, he laughed out loud and extended his hand. "You must be Jeni. It's a pleasure."

"Obviously the pleasure is mine," she said in her saucy way. Twice he pulled me close as though having a hard time believing I was there.

"Yes, I'm here. I told you there wasn't anything to worry about," I said under my breath.

"I was never worried, but I'm glad to have you back."

The trip passed in companionable banter as Brandan told us about things that had been going on in the short time I'd been gone. "After all of the work that was done before you left, you will probably think the place is a mess," he said, "but Miles should be there by now, and he and I will be at your disposal to uncrate furniture, get rid of debris, and rearrange as you see fit. By the end of the day, it should be a lot less confusing. Figured you didn't want to spend the whole time Jeni's here climbing over boxes."

"Always the considerate Brandan. Thank you." Yep, I had taken the plunge. He was a keeper.

"I had them leave the dumpster for an extra week so there's someplace to go with the trash. I can't wait for you to see it," he said.

"You sure he doesn't have a brother?" Jeni piped in from the back.

"Not any you'd want to know," he said, a little too somberly. "But there's no shortage of good men around. We'll see what we can scrounge up for you."

"I'm only here for a few days, but thanks for the offer. And I'm pretty good at the scrounging part."

Pulling up in front of the house took my breath away. Gun-metal gray had been replaced with beautiful hues of yellows and greens. "Oh, my God, Brandan! Isn't it gorgeous?!" I asked, throwing my arms around his neck as we stood in the driveway looking at the transformation that had taken place while I was gone. "Do you love it as much as I do?"

"I think Jordan certainly knows what she's talking about," he said cryptically. "I have to admit I was impressed as it began to take shape, and knew you'd be thrilled. It doesn't even look like the same place."

Miles was standing in the kitchen behind a stack of boxes. "Hey, Jordan, wasn't sure you'd come back, and wondered what the hell I'd do with all this stuff if you didn't. Did you love the outside? I am so glad to see you," he said, hugging me. He straightened with a grin . . . then froze. Having no idea what he could be staring at, I looked behind me to see Jeni with the same stunned expression.

Looking between them, then exchanging a smile with Brandan, I said, "This is my friend Jeni. Jeni, meet Miles."

No response from either as they continued to stare. "Hello? Hello? Anybody home?" I said teasingly, waving my hand in front of Miles' face. "Oh, excuse my manners," he said, "I'm Miles."

Jeni said nothing. It may have been the first time I'd seen her speechless as she continued to hold Mile's hand. Brandan broke the ice. "Hey, Miles, I want to show Willow Tree to Jordan. Would you mind entertaining Jeni till we get back?"

"Hmmm? Oh, sure. Jeni can help me unpack dishes. That okay with you?" he asked.

"Sure," Jeni said, seemingly mesmerized.

We wondered if either of them knew that we'd left or where we'd gone. "And no racing. There are boxes everywhere."

"How did you know that's what I was thinking?" I said. "Okay, tell me what you've done – I mean, besides the obvious."

"Rather than tell you, I'd much rather show you," he said as he unlocked the door to Willow Tree.

Now I felt like Jeni—stunned to silence. Transformed into an elegant tree house, it was every fairy tale come true. "How did you know?" I asked, almost in tears.

"We talked about what you had in mind, and I found some magazines you marked with tabs. I noticed there was a general theme. Miles helped me with this room because I wanted it done before you got back, but I won't ever tell him about the passage. That's your story to tell if you ever want to, not mine."

The care and concern that went into making the room magical was obvious. The four poster bed that stood between the window and armoire was made from tree trunks that were still in their raw shape. "They're willow trees," he said, taking my hand.

The love behind it overwhelmed me more than the magic. "There's no possible way you could have gotten all of this done in the short time I was gone."

"Leave it to you to be practical," he said. "I've actually been conferring with Callie for the past few weeks, getting her input, having her order what I needed. And I worked on the bed at my place and brought it here as soon as the floors were finished."

There was a soft canopy that connected each of the bed posts, with netted drapes tied back. The entire bed would be enclosed in soft material when they were untied. "Callie's idea, not mine. I did the construction, Callie did the decorating, and had a great time doing it, I might add, all the while having contractions. I thought we were going to deliver a baby in here."

"How exciting! Has she had her yet?"

"Talked to Jack this morning. No news."

On either side of the doorway was what appeared to be a real tree that had been cut in half and attached to the wall. "I thought it would give you more of a feeling of actually being in a tree house. Oh, and look at this," he said, pushing a switch. "You can control this from the bed. Callie thought you'd like it." Hundreds of tiny lights illuminated the netting and bed frame.

"It's enchanting." I threw my arms around him and squeezed.

"I'm glad you like it, but you haven't seen most of it yet. Come on," he said, leading me down the stairs to the other end of the hallway. We could hear Miles and Jeni laughing in the kitchen as he opened the door to my office.

On the facing wall was the desk with the chair I'd ordered before I left, a floor-to-ceiling bookcase, and to my right were two overstuffed chairs with a standing lamp. "Callie picked out the chairs, called it a welcome-home present. Said you're welcome to exchange them if they don't suit you."

"They're perfect. I can do a lot of reading in this chair," I said, running my fingers over the soft material. Looking around at the pleasing room with its polished oak floors and beautiful rug, something seemed different. "The room seems smaller? Is that because it has furniture in it?"

"You see things others don't. It *is* smaller. I had Miles build a new wall. He thought I was crazy, but I didn't bother explaining it to him. We've done a lot for each other over the years without asking questions. He knew this was one of those times. There's something I want to tell you."

"Sounds serious."

"I debated about this. You said on too many occasions you wished there was a way for you to have a bathroom up here. I plotted and planned and didn't want to presume, but I made some decisions that maybe I shouldn't have without you. After I did, I felt guilty thinking you needed to be able to trust me, and I'm not sure this is how to go about it. But it's done, and if you don't like it, we'll figure something out."

Now I was intrigued. "Not sure whether to be excited or afraid, but I'm ready."

He pulled something inside the bookcase and the door swung open against the outside wall. He stepped through the opening and motioned me in. Behind the bookshelf was an oasis. The lower half of the walls was wainscoting, the upper an inviting blue. The bathtub appeared to have been carved from a tree trunk, then lined with enamel, and the sink and toilet were against the far wall. The wall to the left appeared to be an inset wall that was covered with the wainscoting from floor to ceiling. The room was literally breathtaking.

"I shared the color with Callie and she selected towels and rugs, but no one else has seen it. I have finishing touches to do, but I hope you're not angry."

"It's staggering. If your intention was to make sure I'd never go back to New York, you've succeeded admirably. Why on earth did you think I'd be mad?"

"Maybe you don't realize where we are. The back half with the sink is your secret room. I used the wainscoting for the lower half, but thought it would be too dark if I didn't break it up with color. The original closet is still there, and," he said, closing the bookcase so we were enclosed in the room, "when that's shut, you have light from the window."

"So you're telling me I can access this from my bedroom bookcase?"

"Yeah, it opens directly into this room like it always did, only now the room is larger. I took down the original wall, laid subflooring, then tiled it. I thought long and hard before I did it and preserved as much as possible. The secret passage and hidden closet are still here, the rest was wasted space. For you to live here comfortably, you needed to have your own bathroom, not be sharing downstairs. And for you to have an office, this was the only realistic alternative."

I pushed on the bookcase I knew to be there, stepped into the bedroom and closed it, leaving Brandan inside. Lifting the middle shelf, the door swung open again. Brandan hadn't moved, but continued to look at me intently. I saw the bright, usable bathroom with the door to the office on the far side. I saw the secret closet no one would know was there.

"I have a favor to ask," I said, crossing my arms and staring directly at him.

"Yes," he said in his two syllable way.

"In the future, I want to be consulted over something so important."

CHAPTER 26

I saw his shoulders slump. "Jordan, I'm so sorry . . ."

"No, let me finish," I said, holding up my hand. "You took a huge chance on something that was incredibly special to me. I loved this room and I loved the things it represented about Edward and his Jordan. It was our secret, yours and mine, and I cherished it for that reason also."

He looked forlorn as I stood in front of him. "It was a huge risk you took, but it paid off." I saw the light in his eyes change. "I'm not unreasonable, and if we'd discussed it beforehand, I would have agreed with all of it and more. You've preserved it as much as possible, but made it a perfect solution to something I desperately needed. Something that, every time I walk into this room, will remind me of the care you take of me."

I looked around the room at what he'd accomplished in such a short time. "And it will remind me what a stud you are that you got it done by yourself, and much more, in less than a week. I'm impressed."

"Miles worked on the new wall while I fixed your room. You said all you needed was a desk and comfy chair, so I figured you didn't need too much more space than what's here. And Callie had so much to do with the final look of your room."

"Will you stay here tonight then?" I asked, putting my arms around his waist.

"Not until it's just you and me and whatever ghosts inhabit this place," he said, covering my lips with his as his beautiful hands surrounded my neck. "And I promise that any surprises like this will be mutually agreed upon beforehand in the future. I'm sorry."

"I'm over it. Just needed a few minutes to absorb that our room is gone, but I'll never be sorry because this replaced it. Thank you."

"You two get lost up there?" Miles called from the lower level.

"Coming!" we called out simultaneously, stepping through the bookcase into my new sanctuary. Brandan opened the door and stood back for me to pass. As I crossed in front of him he took my wrist, raised it to his lips and said, "Consider it a labor of love," as we headed downstairs.

Had he just told me he loved me? I couldn't ask because Miles was coming up the stairs. "Callie had her baby," he said.

"*Really!?* When, where, how much did she weigh?" I asked, thrilled.

"Hold on, hold on, Charlotte Rose was born at 3:42 p.m. in Boulder, weighed seven pounds eight ounces, twenty one inches long, mother and baby doing well."

"What a beautiful name," Jeni said.

"Isn't it? Charlotte after Callie's mom, Rose after Sam's first wife, the namesake of the Amber Rose. Nice tribute to them both. And they're going to call her Charlotte Rose, no nickname. I'm so excited for them."

"She should be home tomorrow," Miles said.

"We'll get some meals prepared so she doesn't have to think about cooking for a while. That'll be fun and I have the perfect kitchen to work in."

Brandan hugged me and kissed the top of my head. "I love your heart."

"So what do you think, ma'am?" Miles asked, referring to my new room.

"I don't want to leave it. It's the most magnificent tree house I've ever seen. Come here, Jeni. You're not going to believe this!"

"Can I bring my sandwich?" she asked, coming up the stairs. "Miles made us something to eat. Handy guy you got here," she said as she passed by him. He and Brandan exchanged a silent look, and Miles shook his head imperceptibly. It would have gone undetected if I hadn't been looking directly at him.

"Wait 'til you see what Brandan and Miles did while I was gone," I said, pulling her the rest of the way. "You're gonna die."

The men disappeared down the hallway as Jeni shrieked with delight when I opened my bedroom door. "No wonder you don't want to stay in New York. *Look* at this! It's the most spectacular, enchanting, inviting, alluring, comforting room I've ever seen!"

"Ah, spoken like someone who does advertising. Oh! Which reminds me, I want you to be thinking about an ad campaign. You'll handle it, of course. I have lots of ideas, but I'm sure they won't compare to what you come up with. Deal?"

"Are you kidding? Of course it's a deal! I've already got brilliant plans percolating. In the meantime, let's find the guys. Shit, Jordan, why didn't you tell me about Miles?"

"How could I possibly have known you would like a *nice* guy?" I said, teasing her.

"He's genuinely nice? Well, that puts the kibosh on *that* then."

"You're kidding, right?"

"Nice guys don't like me, you know that."

"I didn't see Miles running the other way, silly, and he's the best."

"He's pretty hot stuff, but I'm not looking. My life's on overload—my mom taking care of my grandmother whose dementia gets worse daily. I've been trying to land a huge contract forever. If we get it, it'll put us on the map. You know things are rough when packing and moving is an enjoyable vacation."

"But it was fun, wasn't it? We've had a lot of good memories over the years. Come on. Let's go see what mess they're talking about."

"Ah, Brandan, you weren't kidding," I said, walking into room. "Wow, look at this stuff."

"Tell me about it," Miles said, "and most of it's in The Library downstairs."

"Unless we knew exactly where it went," Brandan said, "we stacked boxes in there. We'll take them to the appropriate room as you open them, but I'd like to get the big furniture unpacked first, then we can distribute."

"Great," I said. "You guys help with the big stuff, then we'll be able to do the boxes as we get around to them. This is The Speakeasy, Jeni. It'll be brocades, heavy curtains, mysteriously dark as opposed to depressing. Each room will have a unique mood. Take note, Ms. Ad Exec."

"Oh, I am, I am, trust me," Jeni said, looking around.

When I noticed them staring at each other again, I said, "I have an idea. Brandan and I can take one room, you two take another, and we'll get it done twice as fast. That way each room will have brawn and brains in it."

Brandan laughed out loud, but our friends didn't seem to hear anything. "Guys!" I said, stepping between them, "stop staring and get to work. We have a lot to do and then we can relax. You two take The Snow Drop and get the bed put together. When you get there, Jeni, think stark whites with silver or purple or ice blue highlights. Now shoo."

We could hear them chattering as they headed down the hall. "Do you suppose they heard a word we said?" I asked.

"No idea, but we'll get it done if they don't." He started setting up the bed-frame.

"I wanted to ask you about the look that passed between you and Miles earlier when he shook his head. What was that about?"

"You don't miss a beat, do you?"

"I try to observe what's going on around me. Come on, spill it."

"We have a lot of guys on the crew, most who've been with each other for a long time. Anytime we go into people's houses or are working on a new building site, it's not uncommon for a woman to come on to one of them. If one of us sees someone paying too much attention, we have a signal to ask whether or not they want intervention so things don't get messy, and to make sure someone doesn't get their feelings hurt unnecessarily. Miles made it quite clear he didn't need anyone rescuing him."

"I've known Jeni for a lot of years," I said as we set the box spring and mattress on the newly assembled frame. "I've seen her in a lot of situations, but I can't say I've ever seen her react to a guy like that. Amazing . . ."

"Miles either. He's been so busy with his mom he hasn't shown an interest in anyone in a long time."

"Whatever it is, it would be nice for a guy with a heart to pay attention to her. She's sure known some creeps."

"They don't get much better than Miles. He'd give you the shirt off his back in the middle of winter."

"I think he'd give her the shirt off his back right this minute. Let's go find them."

They had finished the first room and were working on the second. "Okay, this is The Big Apple," I said. "I'm *sure* you'll be able to figure this one out."

"Love it!" she said.

"Look how much room there is when the boxes are out! This is great! Do one more room and we'll do one more room and we'll be done with this for a while."

"Slave driver," Jeni said, and they both cracked up laughing. It was humorous to be around them.

The wind picked up and a freezing drizzle had started as Brandan and I finished carrying empty boxes to the dumpster. I was cold as we came into the parlor, and noticed for the first time some of the furniture that had arrived. "How did I not see this before? Brandan, it's *beautiful*. Can we sit in front of a fire and warm up?"

"Yep. I ran a gas line to this one and the one in the dining room. Figured you didn't want to be hauling and chopping wood and cleaning ashes during winter. With the push of a button, you have instant fire and warmth. Voila," he said as flames flashed on.

"Oh, that's delightful!" Jeni said as she and Miles came into the room. Lightning and thunder were cracking outside, and it looked to be a perfect night for being cozy.

"Do we have anything in the 'fridge?" I asked Brandan as I jumped from another bolt of lightning.

"The ever-faithful Sam brought some up today. Knew what a distraction you'd have walking into this mess, and knew Jeni was coming. I'll help you fix it."

"No, Brandan," Jeni said, "you sit and relax. I'll help Jordan. You guys have done so much, we'll be right back."

CHAPTER 27

"Who knew you'd be magnet and steel?" I said.

"Damn, girl, he's the prettiest thing I've ever laid eyes on," she said, pulling out plates. "Let's hurry so we can get back in there. I could sit and look at him for hours."

Dinner was another memory in the making. We laughed 'til our sides hurt in front of the blazing fire. "So I've often wondered," Jeni said. "We know Wiley Riley would've had a good story to explain your absence, but how did he explain the fact that his only daughter and leading litigator left town abruptly?"

"Oh, you know Father. I inherited a large plantation out West, and it was so extensive and there were so many employees I had to oversee it to make sure it was running properly."

"Oh, I love that man. The most honest liar I've ever met."

"Well, it wasn't actually a lie," Brandan said. "At one time we probably had twenty-five or thirty people working on different aspects of the rehab, and Jordan was technically in charge of them all." That produced a laugh from all of us.

We toasted to another good story before we called it a night. "If this weather keeps up, we'll probably have icy snow in the morning," Brandan said.

"Do you guys want to stay? It's not as though there aren't plenty of rooms," I suggested.

"Rather than heading back to Sugarloaf, what would you think if I stayed in the cottage tonight?" Miles asked.

"No problem, except we have sheets and blankets in here. We can unpack some and you can stay in one of the rooms."

I saw a smile cross Jeni's face, but I wasn't her keeper. She was a big girl, she could do what she wanted. "How about you, Brandan, wanna stay?"

"No, I'm gonna head on out. You girls have Miles to protect you, but I'll be back bright and early."

Jeni looked surprised but headed to The Library to look through boxes for sheets. I walked Brandan to the back door, remembering all that had happened today. "I can't seem to take it all in. Willow Tree is magnificent, and thank you seems so inadequate," I said, hugging him. "Sure you won't stay?"

"You're too much of a temptation, so I'm not staying until Jeni's gone. Not gonna change my mind. If it's going to be unforgettable, I don't want to worry about anyone else hearing you."

"Hearing me? Delicious thought. I'll hold you to that promise," I said breathlessly, kissing him for all I was worth. "Under those circumstances, I'm gonna have to hurry her out of here."

"By the way, I put the journal in the armoire in case you're looking for it. The key's on a tiny nail on the back of the top right headboard. I'll see you in the morning," he said, kissing me one last time. "Hope you enjoy your new room."

I headed to The Library to help look through boxes. "Which room, Miles? Any preference?"

"How about The Gables? I think it's my favorite with the slanted ceilings, and the bed's made up already. I just need some sleep. Needless to say, it's been a long day."

"Needless to say, indeed. I put Jeni in The Big Apple, which is my old room. I'm gonna take The Snow Drop."

"What?" they said in unison, looking at each other.

"You're not gonna sleep in your new room?" Jeni asked. "Oh, sweetheart, why not?"

"Just not ready. I will in a few days." I'd decided I wouldn't stay there until Brandan stayed with me, but I wasn't sharing that information. I wanted the whole thing to be a new experience.

"You staying down here for my sake, Jord?" Jeni asked when Miles left the room.

"Of course not. Don't be silly. I'm not your chastity belt and you're a big girl. I just want to wait a few days before I stay up there. Let Brandan finish everything he needs to do. I'm not gonna rain on your parade."

"No parade. I just had the idea you thought you might have to protect me."

"Not at all. I want a good night's sleep, and it'll be fun to try out the mattresses the guests are gonna use." Hugging her, I said, "Good night, Jeni. I'm so glad to have you here. Thanks for all your help." I shut the door. She and Miles could stay wherever they wanted.

"He's nicer than anyone I've ever known. We talked for a long time in front of the fire after you went to bed, and he didn't even try to kiss me," Jeni said the next morning as we fixed French toast. There were a few inches of snow on the ground, and the guys would be hungry in a bit. Jeni and I had learned how to make French toast when we lived in our first apartment together, and it became our go-to, fast and easy, delicious breakfast treat.

"Things are so different here, aren't they?" I asked wistfully.

"I can understand how you would take this over the crush of New York. Let's get as much done today as possible so we can play tomorrow. And when we're done, maybe we can look at some of the dresses you found."

The day passed in a blur of activity. There was fun and laughter and lots of hard work, and by the end of the day it looked like we'd lived there for months and not just the few hours it had taken. As we stood in the main room looking at what we'd accomplished, Jeni said, "My grandmother often said, 'Many hands make light work.' We sure proved that today. Look at this place, what a thing of beauty. I'm not sure I could leave it either."

"Then don't. Why don't you stay?" I asked in all seriousness.

"Great idea, but no way. My mom could never take care of my grandmother without me. I had to make a lot of future promises to be able to make this trip. Can't envision what leaving would look like."

"I'm sorry you're going through this."

"Thanks. I'm impressed that Miles took that kind of time off to take care of his mother."

"He's remarkable," I said, looking up to see Brandan standing in the doorway.

"You ladies want to go out tonight or stay in?"

"We're going out tomorrow night and I've had a vat of spaghetti stewing all day," I said, "so definitely here. We'll christen the dining room. I even got the candles unpacked. It'll be fun."

I would remember for a long time the laughter and joy and sharing and friendship at the table that night.

꧁ ꧁ ꧁

"Don't be silly, let me come to you. Good grief, Callie, you had a baby four days ago."

"Charlotte Rose and I have errands to run, and I have a Boba wrap. Keeps her warm and keeps me hands free. And I feel fantastic. If you're going to be around, we should be there about noon, if that's okay? I can't wait to see your progress. We'll get you on the cover of Homes Illustrated yet."

"You were a huge part of it. Your ideas were perfect. I can't wait to show you around and see the baby. My best friend is here from New York, so it's perfect."

I had special treats and herb tea ready when she got there. "You look fantastic!" I said. "And she looks so comfortable wrapped up like that! It must feel like being in the womb, next to her mama's heart, all cocooned."

"It's an amazing invention. Of course something like this has been around forever, but someone took a good idea and ran with it. Good marketing," Callie said.

"Speaking of which, I want you to meet my friend, Jeni. She owns an ad agency in the City."

"So nice to meet you. What do you think of Jordan's place here? A little different than what you're used to, I suspect."

"I've never seen anything like it, frankly. She deserves it."

"Oh, Jordan, what you've done is gorgeous! And you were so right about the yellow! I'm planning on promoting Madeline Manor to my clients who come in from out-of-state. And how did you like *your* room? Pretty fantastic, huh?"

"I can't describe how that room affects me. You've got remarkable vision."

"I just helped with the details, Brandan had the real ideas. No wonder he and Jack work so well together. Who did you end up hiring to be your Innkeeper?"

"Joey seemed to be the best candidate. Lots of initiative, good cook, innovative ideas. It seemed like a good match."

"He's a great choice."

"I'm so glad you think so! And, just to let you know, I've decided to take the Colorado Bar when things settle down," I said, deciding to put a voice to my decision.

"Fantastic! I told you there's a pull here that's hard to ignore. Oh, that makes me happy! And I'll be your first client. That'll work out splendidly!" she said, giving me a big hug.

I'm not sure exactly who I felt like as we pressed into the crowd at the Pioneer Inn, but I knew I looked sensational in my authentic 1920s flapper dress that was part of the find in the armoire. Jeni selected a mid-calf 1940s style and was stunning.

Brandan and Miles were going to meet us, and we slipped through the crowd, exchanging pleasantries and getting wolf whistles as we passed. Heading to the back room, I could smell the beer and lingering smoke on the clothes of the patrons as I looked for Brandan in the dim orange light. My stomach clinched as I spotted him in the far corner with a woman's hands tenderly touching his face. He was leaning into her with her lips near his ear.

While my immediate reaction was to think of Andrew, this was not at all the same feeling. Seeing Andrew had produced a sense of shock and surprise, but it didn't hurt like this, didn't stab the heart with the same intensity, didn't make me immediately want to run and collapse. I didn't know who she was in her Pocahontas wig and skimpy leather, but she looked like she and Brandan were close. I could feel the bile rise in my throat from watching what appeared to be an intimate exchange. Brandan stood with his arms around her, then leaned to hear something she was saying. With her hands on his face, she kissed him on the lips as I turned hurriedly away.

Looking back one more time, I saw him kissing her tenderly on the forehead. I couldn't watch anymore, and needed desperately to be out of the crush of the pressing throng.

"I've got a splitting headache," I said in a loud voice that Jeni could barely hear over the din of the rowdy mob and jukebox. "Enjoy yourself. You look like a million bucks."

"I'll come with you! Is there anything I can do to help?"

"Of course you won't come with me, silly. Stay. Enjoy. Go find Miles and let him see what a knockout you are. I'll see you in the morning."

"What about Brandan?"

I pretended I hadn't heard as I threaded my way through the burgeoning horde. The cold night air slapped at me as I hurried up the hill. It was a friendly town, but I pulled my knife out of my garter to have it ready as I tried desperately not to think of the tender look I had seen on Brandan's face . . . a look intended for someone else. The pain was so much worse than Andrew, and I wasn't sure I would make it home before I broke down. How could I have been so foolish—again?

CHAPTER 28

This hurt so much. I leaned against the door, taking deep breaths. Jeni would be worried about me, so I scribbled a note to let her know where I was, and made it to the room that was the fulfillment of every imaginable dream before I broke down. The sobs came deeply and painfully. I threw myself on the bed without turning on lights and cried until I was spent. Jeni would call them 'ugly tears.'

I was so deeply asleep I didn't feel him when he laid next to me, pulling me into his arms. Sometime in the night I became conscious of his warm body and put my arms around him, holding him close. Then I remembered why I was here and moved away from him.

"Is your headache gone? Can I help you out of your beaded dress so you sleep better?"

"What you can do is get out . . . now."

I saw the surprise on his face, even saw a look that appeared to be hurt.

"What happened, Digger? What's the matter?"

"Don't you dare 'Digger' me . . . just get out."

"In what may be an unfortunate turn of events for you, you've found yourself saddled with someone who won't walk away easily. So scream and yell and throw things all you want, or better still, just talk rationally, but I'm not leaving until you tell me what's going on," he said, sitting up, leaning against the headboard.

"Did you think I wouldn't see you kissing Pocahontas? Did you think just because it was dark I wouldn't notice your tender kiss, the way you were holding her in your arms?" I said, almost yelling. And then I sobbed again. "Just go. Leave me alone."

He was on his knees on the bed in a heartbeat, taking me in his arms, kissing my face with the tears streaming. "I'm so sorry you saw that. It must've been painful, but you have to know I'm not Andrew, and you've got it all wrong," he said, pulling me down and wrapping his arms around me.

"Don't sweet talk me, Brandan," I said as I tried to sit up. "Just go. I know what I saw, just go."

"For a lawyer lady, you're not very sharp sometimes. Can you truly believe what you saw is the truth?"

"I've seen it before. I'm familiar with that kind of truth."

"There are different truths, and while you saw something you convinced yourself was truth, you're wrong. I've lived most of my life believing a lie, and I won't let you go another minute without telling you what you *actually* saw."

Could I believe him, whatever he was going to tell me? Hadn't I been here? No, it hadn't hurt like this before, and I never cared what Andrew's excuse was.

"I'm sorry you saw us before you saw me, Jordan. I was talking to April—she was Pocahontas."

"But you were kissing her." Even in my own ears I sounded pitiful.

"She kissed me good-bye. She finally realized it was never going to work out with me, so she's dating someone from town. She wanted me to know she was letting go. She'd had a few drinks, and she probably said more than she intended. Gabe was my best friend and I pulled him out of the water. She was pregnant and scared, and I was a lifeline and tangible. She had me so wrapped up in her mind with Gabe and his death. She held on tightly to me because she knew when she let go, it also meant, to her, she'd be letting go of him."

I was filtering his words. My heart broke for April, it must've been so difficult. My head was resting on his chest, his arms around me. "Go on," I whispered.

"When we gave James Gabriel the photo, she said something clicked and she finally understood Gabe wasn't coming back, and she was able to let go of me. I was happy for her. It was genuine affection you saw me sharing with her. I've known her since we were kids and it hurt me to hurt her, but I didn't know what else to do without being cruel."

"I should have waited to find out, but honestly it never occurred to me. I'm so good at looking at both sides of any given situation, but I must have tunnel vision when it comes to my personal life. I'm sorry, I only saw what my brain registered. I couldn't believe I'd been so blind again."

He tilted my head and kissed me. "My whole life was based on a lie, and I saw misguided love destroy my mother. Even though I felt the guilt and tried to shoulder the responsibility, it was never good enough. I vowed I would never let a woman close enough that she could hurt me like that. The minute they said 'I love you' or wanted more than what I was offering, I found the quickest exit to get rid of them. No entanglements, no crap like I'd grown up with, no exceptions."

I listened to his soothing voice, and knew there was no doubt he was telling me the truth about April. I had overreacted, and I trusted this man.

"And then I met you."

I stilled.

"You changed all preconceived notions of what I wanted my life to look like. You upended my world in a short time, and I knew I couldn't let you go, ever. I understood what April was saying about Gabe. I can't picture, even now, losing you. I love all of you—your heart, your brains, your ability, your tenderness—to say nothing of how my body reacts to yours," he said.

"What I'm telling you so inadequately is that I intend to make you mine. I want you as my wife, I want you as the mother of our children, I want there to come a time you love me anywhere near the degree I love you. I'm giving you fair warning, when this happens between us, there'll be no going back."

I was wordless, exhausted. The emotional roller coaster of the evening was close to crashing. His words were sincere, believable. Was I ready to commit to something like he was suggesting after only these few months, and after what had happened with Andrew? He had knocked me off kilter.

"Jeni will be gone tomorrow afternoon," he continued. "I'm so ready for you, for the next phase to begin. I'm sorry you were hurt tonight, but there's not another woman in my life. It's only you."

Andrew's taunt last week of never having loved me came to mind. I believed I was a lot more aware now than with Andrew, and nothing about Brandan gave me pause, even when looking at it objectively. "Will you stay tonight?" I asked, almost asleep.

"Let's get your dress off so you can sleep comfortably. Have you enjoyed sleeping up here?"

"I don't know, I haven't done it yet."

"Why not?" he asked, helping me to my feet.

"Because I didn't want to stay up here without you," I said with a yawn, my only contributing action was to raise my arms as he lifted the dress above my head.

He paused at my words, studying my sleepy face. He picked me up and laid me on the bed, pulling the covers over us. "I'm glad you're as tired as you are. It'll make it slightly easier on my aching body to not take you tonight. I'll stay for a while."

But I didn't hear him. I was asleep.

The smell of bacon woke me, and I wondered if Jeni was already awake. Putting on comfortable clothes, I went barefoot to the kitchen. "If you're gonna keep taking care of me like this, I may have to keep you around," I said, hugging him from behind.

"If bacon is what'll do it, I'll buy a herd of pigs," he said.

"Thanks for last night. Thank you for staying and explaining. I'm sorry I jumped to conclusions, but I'm glad for April. That was a big step," I said, pouring coffee.

"I'm glad you understand. Last night I felt like I got my old friend back, and maybe a burden had been lifted from her. She should be better now, which'll be good for all of them."

"I'm gonna leave here about eleven to take Jeni. I'll be back mid-afternoon, then I want to see if I can find out anything about Willow. It's crazy how she just disappeared."

"My plan is to finish Willow Tree so that will be out of your way."

"May I mention again how blown away I am about it all? Magical, and then you open the door and see the bathroom and nothing about it feels real. I probably stood there five minutes this morning admiring it."

"I'm glad you like it. Lots of love went into the building of it," he said, kissing my forehead, then setting a plate in front of me. "Eat up, you're gonna need your strength for later."

The morning passed in a whirl. Jeni and I had a wonderful trip to the airport. The consummate gentleman, Miles had only kissed her lightly as they said their good-byes, but his embrace spoke volumes.

Jeni said dreamily, "Nothing narcissistic about him. And what he's been through is so tragic. He gave me

awesome insight, and nothing more than a kiss—
remarkable."

"Offer's always open here," I said again.

"Not gonna happen, but it's a great thought. What a
hunk. And you know what, Jord? He's so much more
than just a pretty face. He's kind and considerate and
capable and charming and . . ."

"Yep, you got bitten. There are some mighty fine
people in town. I'm anxious to see how it plays out."

"As much as possible, I want to be a part of it. I love
it here, but too many responsibilities at home to think
about anything else right now."

"You know you can visit any time."

Every part of me got butterflies at the thought of
tonight. The time had arrived, and I was eager. But
that was hours away, and I planned on immersing
myself in finding out what I could about my great
grandmother. It was frustrating that I lost her trail,
but I had in-depth resources, and I wouldn't stop until
I figured it out.

Three hours in front of the computer had me ready
to call it quits for the day—until I ran across an article
from a 1917 newspaper that a Willow Stratton
married Walter Henry Ray. But her name hadn't been
Stratton. This was a huge part of the missing piece I'd
been looking for. She was born Willow Harriman in
1894 to Jordan and Andrew Harriman, so somewhere
along the way she had taken Edward's name. Oh,
Edward, my heart ached for them all.

"Any progress, Digger?" Brandan said, nuzzling my
neck.

"Yes and no. But the more I learn, the more
confused I get. Hey, why are you so wet?"

"Started to rain. Actually, it's more like ice needles
than rain, but it still leaves you wet and freezing."

"We'll warm you up in a minute," I said, kissing his lips. "The biggest shock of the day is that Willow was *not* my great-grandmother. She was my great-great-aunt. Adelaine was, in fact, my great-grandmother's name, and Willow was her sister. I finally found Willow, but she had a different last name in the records—Willow Stratton—which was Edward's last name, but she was born as Willow Harriman and I've got a lot of digging still to do to figure it out. I'm hoping some of the paperwork from the trunk will give us more answers."

Surrounding me with his arms, he said, "You're not thinking of doing that tonight are you?" He placed gentle kisses on my lips, my neck, my ear.

"Thinking of doing what?" I sighed, allowing the sensations his lips were causing to have free reign. "I'm only thinking of doing one thing tonight." My head was back, my neck exposed when he stilled.

"You sure?"

"Never been more sure of anything," I whispered, meeting his gaze.

CHAPTER 29

"Wanna try out the new shower?" I asked. "Race you." I took the stairs two at a time, but he didn't take the bait. He walked into the room leisurely. I was so aware of him, of everything about him. I could almost feel the softness of his well-worn shirt as he unbuttoned it, feel the smoothness of his hands that were such a dichotomy to the work he did with them.

He lifted the middle shelf. "Tonight I'm saving my energy for you," he said, turning on both shower heads, then stepping out of his pants. "Join me?"

"You don't have to ask twice," I said, breathless from the run and the sight of his body as he undressed.

Pulling my clothes off on the way, we stared at each other. He held me in the warm stream of water. "You're a contradiction to me," I whispered. "There's nothing you can't do. You're as strong and tough as anyone, but full of such gentleness."

"I'm not sure how to say it, but I appreciate your appreciation of the things I do. Makes me want to do more, and somehow it's a real turn on."

I could feel him grow hard against me. Rather than quench the fire, the spray from the shower ignited it, my body reacting to the flames. My hands roamed his chest and my tongue circled his taut, wet nipple. He groaned as he protected me from the spray, bending to take my lips. Our mouths were slick from the splashing drops, and the moist, sliding sensation of lip against lip promised of things to come.

"I've never waited for another woman," he said, intensifying his hold. "I'm not sure I can wait much longer."

"No need," I said softly against his lips as his hand found its way to my thighs and the core of my desire. I groaned as his finger entered me, and I wanted him, all of him. "I want you too much to play in here anymore," I said, pulling him harder against my lips with my fingers threading through his hair. "I need you—now."

The water was off in an instant. "Now it is."

The next few minutes were intimate as we dried each other. I couldn't believe this existed in real life. It was the stuff of fairy tales as he followed me to the bed. He turned on a strand of twinkling lights, and the room took on an ethereal quality.

"When Callie and I installed the lights, I saw this moment. I wanted it to be special, something you would never forget."

"Like there's anything that could make me forget?"

He started at my neck and worked his way to my sensitive breast. His tongue was doing delicious things, swirling, pulling, as his hand moved lower, gently touching, moving, exciting, drawing me out. When his lips followed the trail, I raised my hips to meet him. Our eyes met, "Don't stop," I said, "please, don't stop."

Without saying a word, his tongue found my need, probing, pulling, moving back and forth, hard then soft, then gentle again. I knew I was making noise, I was moving in controlled rhythm with the movement of his tongue, and I was primed. "Now—please. We have plenty of time to make slow, sweet love—tomorrow. Tonight, I'm impatient. We've waited so long. Please, Brandan."

He kissed his way up my body, his tongue finding my navel, then each breast, then the sensitive area at the base of my neck. As his lips took mine, I felt possessed—by him, by my feelings, by the setting. I craved him. His kissing took on the rhythm of sex as our bodies danced in tune with each other. He put his warm, hard, wet tip against my opening. I moaned, trying to take him inside me. "Open your eyes, Jordan, look at me." As I opened them, a clap of lightning illuminated the room, followed immediately by the roll of thunder that went on and on.

He closed his eyes momentarily then captured me with his gaze. "How appropriate," he said, continuing to move just the tip in and out, "I was already feeling thunder struck."

"I need you, stop talking and *please* take me. I've waited a lifetime for this."

He continued with his pulsing movement, in and out but not enough for satisfaction, taking breaths as though it were equally hard on him to wait. "You understand what we're doing here? We're not just making love, I'm branding you, I'm making you mine," he said with one deep, hard thrust that had me crying out in pleasure. In a dance as old as time, we moved against each other. I kissed him, wanting the intimacy, the contact, the glide of his lips as he entered me time and again.

The room lit again with nearby lightning. "It always comes before the thunder," he said softly, knowing I was close, ready to break apart with me. As I unraveled, as this new experience had me contracting and whispering his name, pulling me deeper under his spell, the roll of thunder built to such a rumble as to rattle the windows. Looking into each other's eyes, we shattered together, with nature seemingly playing to a crescendo with us.

Minutes passed before he rolled to his back, taking me with him to lie on his chest, kissing my hair, holding me tightly. "Unforgettable."

"Thank you. You have no idea . . . thank you," I said, laughing.

"What's so funny?" he asked, tipping my face to look at me.

"Not only do I now understand why they call it 'the little death,' but I know what all the fuss is about. Good God, Brandan, no way we would have waited this long if I knew what was on the other side."

"Everything in its own time, Digger. We know that better than most."

"We do, don't we?" I said with a yawn. "Thank you, Brandan, I can truthfully say it was worth the wait."

He leaned over and turned off the lights. "I probably won't mention it to Callie, but those were a nice touch."

"Indeed they were," I said, closing my eyes with his arms still around me. "Indeed they were."

The sleet tapping against the window woke me in the wee hours. Still wrapped in Brandan's arms, my hand glided over his chest as it moved lower to wrap my fingers around him. I wasn't sure he was awake as he hardened under my massaging fingers, but his moan turned me on again. I slipped lower under the covers and took him in my mouth, ever so slightly rubbing my teeth against his swelling head, moving my tongue back and forth along his hardening rim.

I leaned over him, gripping his lower shaft in my fist while moving my mouth up and down along the tip. Gently sucking, I was pleased how quickly I wanted him again. I crawled up his body, positioning myself above him. "I think you've created a monster," I whispered, lowering so I was rubbing against him but not taking him inside me. Rocking back and forth over him, he took hold of my thighs.

"I'm not going to last long if you keep doing that," he said, pushing against me.

"Good, because I'm ready. It took me all these years, and now I'm like a kid with a toy. Just the thought of this brings me to the brink," I said, raising and positioning him with my hand at my waiting entrance.

Sliding over him, we both made a noise. Just hearing his pleasure brought such satisfaction. I leaned forward, arms straight, supporting myself as I clenched around him, moving up and down.

"Damn, woman, you sure know what you're doing," he said, meeting me thrust for thrust.

"You bring it out in me," I said, kissing him, all the while milking him.

His hands pulled my face closer, kissing me harder, pushing into me harder, biting my lip in pleasure. "Are you ready?" he said, the simultaneous thrust of his tongue and manhood in rhythm sent me cascading into a trembling mass. My release triggered him, and a few minutes later we were again aware of the tapping of the sleet against the window. "Nowhere I'd rather be than out of the elements, wrapped up with you," he said, rolling partially over so his face was above me.

"It's so much more than physical," he said. "There's something about minds meshing and souls touching. It's almost like our spirits became one. Don't mean to sound mystical, but I feel like it was always meant to be this way between us, like we've come home."

Touched beyond measure, I asked, "How does one as masculine as you have such an incredibly tender heart?"

His lips gently touched my face, my eyes. "I love you. All of my life I thought I wanted to avoid this entanglement, and now I don't want to live without it. Will you marry me?"

I sat up and touched his face. "Give me time, Brandan. There's no doubt I love you, but it's too soon, there's too much that's happened in such a short time. Give me a little while."

"Take all the time you want, but it's not gonna change the outcome. We are what we are, and we're meant to be together. Again I'll say what Edward knew, I'm sorry you were hurt, but I will forever be grateful that things didn't work out with Andrew."

I leaned forward, putting my forehead against his lips. "You know there is no part of me that doubts that, unless I try to rationalize it. In my heart of hearts I know all of this is true, but it's crazy, right? How are we possibly fulfilling some eccentric story that obviously didn't work out a hundred and twenty years ago?"

"Believe it or not, this is about us, not them. It doesn't change just because it doesn't make logical sense. You're a lawyer, you look for the logic in situations. I get it, it's where I've always lived. But sometimes what's under your nose isn't the truth, as in the case of my father. And sometimes what seems absolutely far-fetched, as in our case and Edward's journal, is as real as anything we've known. I'll give you time, but know it's inevitable," he said, pulling on his pants and shirt. "Race you," he laughed, opening the door and sauntering down the stairs.

"*You!*" I said, jumping up to throw on some clothes. There was no contest, he already had the food out by the time I reached the kitchen.

"Looks like it's going to be miserable today. What's on your agenda?"

"I want to find out about Willow, that's my driving goal, and then my next project will be to spend time in the journal."

"No diversions at all?" he asked, leaning over to kiss me. His hand caressed my cheek and found its sensual way to my breast.

"Are you kidding? I'm not gonna be able to walk, much less do that again . . . at least for a while. But check back with me soon," I said, responding kiss for kiss.

CHAPTER 30

"Any progress?" he asked, several hours later, rubbing my aching shoulders.

"Some. I found out Willow had a daughter, Doris Ray Perkins, in 1918, and then I just found out that eight years later she had a second daughter, Virginia Ray Wiltsey. So I feel like I'm making *some* progress. How about you?"

When there was no answer, I looked to see Brandan with a stunned expression on his face. "What's the matter? You look like you've seen a ghost," I said, trying to tease.

"Virginia Ray Wiltsey was . . ." His eyes met mine, "She was my grandmother."

Numbly silent, we stared at each other. "What does that mean, then? Are you and I related?" he asked. "Doesn't matter one way or the other, it was so far back as to not matter, but what's the connection?"

"Okay, let me make this as simple as possible. Edward and Jordan Stratton were married. Jordan got pregnant with Edward's child, Willow, but it appears Edward died before Willow was born. By the time Willow was born, Jordan was married to Andrew Harriman, which makes me physically sick to my stomach."

"So Willow is *my* great-grandmother, the only child of Edward and Jordan?" he asked with a furrowed brow.

"Yes. Then Jordan and Andrew had two more children, which somehow infuriates me, and one of their daughters was *my* great-grandmother Adelaine."

"So our relationship, yours and mine," he worked at piecing it together, "has a common thread of Jordan Stratton Harriman, the original Jordan—me being Edward's great-great-grandchild, you being Andrew's?"

"I'm not sure why I feel like that's such an injustice, but yes, that's right. That would explain why you look just like the pictures of Edward. Isn't it remarkable how genes can pass down over more than a century and be so undiluted?"

We continued to stare. "It has no bearing on us, though, right?" he asked finally.

Surprised at what he must be thinking, I ran my hand up his arm, "Of course not. No way. To me it's absolutely exciting this has come full circle. We don't have enough of a connection that there's more than a drop of shared blood. Actually, the more I think about it, the more I think it's cool. Seriously, we come from the same place, we have the same heritage, we have this crazy connection we couldn't explain to anyone and have them believe us. It blows me away how awesome that is."

Holding me tighter, chin resting on my head, he said, "How did I think I was living before I met you? I love you, Digger. Thank you. For some reason, it was a shock to think we might somehow be related, like there might be something wrong with it."

"Nope. No court in the land would convict us," I laughed, "and it doesn't even make me feel creepy." Putting my cheek against his chest, I said, "Truth be known, there's only one thing that upsets me about all of this."

"What's that?"

"That I'm the offspring of Andrew. I hate Andrew and have no idea why. He may have been a nice guy for all we know, but just hearing his name makes me hiss. Do you suppose he was the same Andrew she was engaged to before she married Edward?"

"Oh, God, I hope not, but you'll find out."

"I *will* find out. It'll eat away at me until I do. I hope the journal sheds some light on it."

"I came in to grab us a bite to eat. Want anything?"

"No, thanks. Right now I just want to read, heal my aching heart." I stood on tiptoe to kiss him as I headed up the stairs. "Does this mean I get to call you 'Cuz'?"

"It doesn't matter what you call me, as long as you love me." Our eyes met. "Speaking of which, Miles was pretty smitten with Jeni. I've been hearing about her virtues this morning."

"That's neat. She was pretty taken with him, too. But her life is so complicated, it might be years before she can untangle it."

"It'll work out if it's meant to."

On my way home, I stopped by the Amber Rose to tell Sam one more time how much I appreciated my Mac truck, as I affectionately thought of it. Who would have known a car that was over five decades old could be so delightful? I was finishing lunch when Sam said, "I hear your mighty handy with a knife."

"Who told you that?"

"James Gabriel," he said. "That kid sure does think you hung the sun an' the moon."

"Thanks, Sam. That gives me a great idea. And thanks for lunch, excellent as usual," I said as I paid my bill and headed to April's house.

"If it's all right with you, I'd like for James Gabriel to come over at times and let me teach him how to whittle. He seems fascinated by it, and I was younger than he is when my grandfather taught me."

"That's so nice of you. He likes you a lot, and it would not only be a diversion for him and give him something to do away from the TV, but it'd give me a little free time now and then."

"I'm looking forward to it. This Saturday? Just send him up whenever. I'll be around."

"Jordan?" April said from the doorway as I was getting into my truck. "Take good care of him. They don't come much better than Brandan."

Did everyone know? Not saying a word, I headed back to the house, thinking about how hard it must have been for her. Like Jordan, she lost the husband she loved when she was pregnant. Not a time you'd want to be alone. I empathized.

That Saturday morning was spent peacefully going over journal entries. "This has become one of my favorite pastimes," he said, handing me a cup of coffee before sitting down. We'd found a pair of large rockers that were perfect at the end of the porch. Barker Reservoir glistened in the distance like diamonds in the sunlight. "I know it sounds strange, but the more we learn, the more I feel like I'm being completed. Hard to explain, but I like hearing you tell me about them."

I set my coffee down and leaned over to take his hand. Kissing his fingertips, I teased him with my tongue. The noise he made encouraged me to take his thumb and start sucking, his four fingers cupping my cheek. "Dear Lord," he said in a low voice, "it's amazing how I can feel your mouth elsewhere when you do that."

I moved to his next finger, sliding it in and out of my mouth, wrapping my tongue around it with each thrust. I stood between his legs and he pulled me closer. Now he was sucking on one of my fingers, doing to me what I had just been doing to him when we heard a sound. Leaning over, lips almost touching, I said, "shhh" as I put my moist finger against his mouth.

James Gabriel came out of the trees and walked onto the porch. "You guys sure do kiss a lot," he said matter of factly, sitting down on a step. "Mama said you're gonna show me how to whipple."

"Whittle," I corrected, "and I'm looking forward to teaching you."

"I'll be right back," Brandan said. A few minutes later, he set a wrapped present in front of James Gabriel. "This is yours. I had it made for you."

Tearing off the wrapping, he removed the top and said, "For *me*?!"

"I figured if you're old enough to whittle, you're old enough to learn how to take care of your own knife."

When James Gabriel threw his arms around Brandan's waist, our eyes met. He must have known what I was thinking because he whispered, "I know. I love you, too."

The next hour was spent collecting wood and teaching him the basics of his knife, how to hold it, how to fold it, how to sharpen it, and how to cut so the blade was pointing away from his body. We made plans for him to come up after school during the week for his next lesson.

"I've got a few supplies to pick up," Brandan said. "I'll be back within the hour."

"And I obviously have some reading I want to do. You'll know where to find me."

Settling in on the bed where I had so recently shared an incredible encounter, I opened Edward's journal.

The snake, Simon Legree, continues to hang around, but Jordan seems oblivious to him. Thank God for that, but I don't trust him. Daily my love for Jordan grows, and I wonder how I ever lived without her. When we are together, it is so much more than physical. There is something about the minds meshing, the souls touching, and the spirits becoming one. It seems mystical, like it was always meant to be this way between us. When we are in each other's arms, it's like being home.

It produced goosebumps as I read almost the identical words Brandan had said to me the night before. I no longer tried to explain it. But who was Simon Legree? Surely that wasn't his real name.

The joy of knowing I will be a father in a few months makes my work more urgent. I must secure the land and mines before Simon finds out. I do not trust him, and will not even tell Jordan until it is accomplished. She would only worry, and I want nothing more than to bring joy to her life. She is my completer, my heart. I wax poetic, but my heart is full to overflowing with the treasure I found, and I'm not speaking about the gold. I was a bitter, cynical man until meeting her. She saved me.

Gold? Edward found gold? I thought he'd been involved in the tungsten mining nearby, but gold? The following day's entry read:

After filing my claim with Joshua Witherspoon at the Boulder Mining Company today, I saw Simon talking to him on my way out of town. I need to warn Jordan that if anything happens to me, Simon will be the one to blame and will make it look like an accident. I know the slime he slithers in. She must be on the lookout if he becomes wealthy. It will be her money he's spending. Maybe she and I can take a trip until things settle down, although knowing my wife, she will not want to leave home until after our baby is born. Jordan is convinced it is a girl and will name her Willow. She won't even consider a boy's name. I pray she is not disappointed.

On my way home today I purchased the first present for our child, a pair of lace-up ice skates. Whether boy or girl, they will fit a child. My fondest memories were those of my mother teaching me to skate on the pond near our home. It is my most vivid memory of her before she died. Any warm emotion left me at her death until the day I met Jordan. I will do anything to bring her wonder.

I wanted to know more. Had Simon actually killed Edward? Was Andrew, in fact, Simon? If that was the case, how could Jordan have even considered marrying him? The thought was abhorrent.

"Okay, what'd you find?" Brandan asked, pulling me close as he sat on the bed.

"Oh, Brandan, there's something so senseless going on. First Edward says almost the identical words you said to me last night, then he talks about knowing he's going to be a father and Jordan is convinced it will be a girl and she named her Willow before she was born and Edward bought her ice skates and Edward's mother died and Edward found gold and believed Simon would kill him for it and he wanted to protect Jordan and . . ."

"Slow down, slow down," he said, taking my face in his hands. "Do we have any idea yet what happened to Edward or who Simon actually is?"

"None whatsoever, but there aren't many days left in the journal, then the paperwork. What if there's no answer?"

"You'll still find the answers. It's who you are. Miles left a while ago, but the snow is falling fast and furious. Do you want me to stay or go?"

"Are you kidding? Was that supposed to be a trick question? I want you here. I'm exhausted but wired."

"Have you had anything to eat today?"

"I don't know. What day is it?" I laughed. "Let's go fix something and call it a night."

The table was set with flickering candles, sandwiches, sliced tomatoes, a few chips, and a bottle of wine. "What's this?" I said, looking back and forth from Brandan to the table. "When did you possibly have time to do *this?*"

"I figured you hadn't eaten and it wasn't hard to throw some things together. You want something else, maybe?" he asked with a grin.

"I want to know where you came from and how'd I get so lucky to find you?"

"It's a two way street."

"How did it go in the cottage today?"

"We've almost got the basics done. It'll be a pretty impressive place when it's cleaned up. Arts and Craft style. Definitely a stand-alone house. Wonder who it was for?"

"When I'm done with the journal, I'll see if I can track it down in county records. Thank you," I said with a yawn, placing my hand on his. "This has been like a dream and you've been the dream maker," I said with another yawn.

"Let's get you up to bed—to sleep. Even *that* is something to look forward to with you in my arms."

CHAPTER 31

When I woke the next morning, the bookcase was open and I could hear the water running. The tub was filling, and I came up behind Brandan and put my arms around his waist. "You taking a bath?"

"No, we hadn't talked about it, but I figured you'd love to soak up to your neck in this tub on a cold morning."

"It's incredibly perfect for this space. What kind of wood is it?"

"Oak, like the wainscoting. I'd seen one before, and when you talked about a fancy tree house it came to mind. I ordered it a month ago and had it sitting in its box in the yard with the rest of the supplies. I know it was a gamble, but I'm glad you like it."

"It's so unique."

"Wait 'til you see Callie's tub at the cabin. *That's* the most incredible tub you'll ever see, but this one's not too bad. And it's perfect, isn't it? I thought I'd shave and get ready for the day while you soak."

"I love that idea!" I said, climbing the two steps into the tub and sinking into its warming welcome. "Thank you for thinking of this. It's a slice of heaven."

"You've mentioned how much you love baths and rarely get to take them, so I hope you get to spend time here. When I installed it, I thought of moments like this, you relaxing and me being able to see you in the mirror while we talk."

"It's perfection, and speaking of talking . . ."

"Yes," he said, drawing it out.

"In the research I've been doing the past weeks, I've found so many branches of the family all over the country. Dozens of them who, like us, were directly related in some manner to the original Jordan, and had families of their own and moved away, and then *they* had families of their own and scattered."

"And what do you want to do with that information?" he asked, holding my gaze.

"Hear me out. I've been thinking how interesting it would be to invite them here." I smiled at his stunned reflection.

"Go on."

"We could send invitations, tell them they could stay as our guest for the weekend, that we've traced a lot of the family history and would love for them to bring photos or letters or memorabilia they might have from their ancestors. Then I'll make copies and give everyone a disc of everything that people share. What do you think of that?"

"Brilliant, Counselor, absolutely brilliant."

"You think so? I'm so glad! I figured we could have everyone meet early next year, maybe February or March? The house should be finished, I'll have had a chance to go through the journal, photos, paperwork."

"I'll do what I can to help."

"I'll send invites to the known offspring at their last known address, and then suggest they let *their* relatives know—ones I don't have record of. As long as we have an idea how many are coming, we should be fine. I'm anxious to hear other people's tales and see how the puzzle pieces fit."

"That's a lot of work for you in the meantime."

"I'm thriving on it right now. I'm sure a time will come when we lay the past to rest," I said, "but I want to know what I can about it before that happens."

"Do you feel a different connection between us today?"

"What do you mean?"

"If someone had told us before that we were related, I'm not sure how I would have reacted. It's so far back it doesn't matter, but there's something so . . . so . . . so appealing, for lack of a better word . . . to think we share a bloodline, even if it's only a smattering. Almost a crazy kind of destiny."

"I feel the same way, like we're connected. Although when I hear myself say it out loud, I have to wonder at my sanity." He pulled his shirt on and was buttoning it as he sat on the edge of the tub.

"Whenever you're done, come on down to the kitchen, I'll fix us a bite. If the truck can make it through in this weather, your movers should be here tomorrow, and we'll get Joey's apartment finished before he starts next week."

"I look forward to feeding *you* in the future. You've been doing most of it, and I want to impress you with my prowess."

"That makes two of us."

The house was finished. Thanksgiving was fast approaching. Our first gala at Madeline Manor would involve my parents, Jeni and her family, along with Miles and Brandan, and Sam from the Amber Rose and his wife Sunni. It would be our first real gathering, and I was looking forward to it and dreading it at the same time. Joey was a great help and had taken much of the burden of the details from me.

Everyone was scheduled to arrive tomorrow. We were enjoying a beautiful autumn, and the weather appeared to be cooperating. "You nervous?" Brandan asked, coming up behind me and putting his arms around my waist as I brushed my hair.

"A little," I confessed, stretching softly as he pressed against me and stroked my breasts.

"Anything I can do to help relax you?" he asked huskily, looking at me in the mirror as he freed my chest from the confines of my robe.

"What you're doing can probably get the job done," I purred, leaning my elbows on the counter, pressing my backside into his hardening crotch. My head was resting on my folded hands, and the sensations of him touching me intimately had me hot and ready.

"Look at me," he said softly, letting my robe fall to the floor.

I opened my eyes to see his reflection. "I want you to see me as I take you," he said, stepping out of his jeans. "I want you to see how much I want you." He was kissing my lower back as his finger entered me, then he stood straight again, his erection visible between us. He rubbed against me, pulling my hips toward him, teasing, preparing.

"For the only time in my life," he said deeply, slowly guiding himself into me, then withdrawing, "I'm in love. I've been waiting for you, I just didn't know it. I've never been possessive about anything before. You're mine. I want you to watch and see how well we fit together," he said, thrusting fully into me.

I watched his image with desire, moving in rhythm until his fingers circled me, rubbing, bringing me to the threshold as he continued to move in and out, pressing on all the right places. "It's my pleasure to bring *you* pleasure," he said deep in his throat, finding the exact spot to coerce as he thrust in a position that made me explode.

Crying out, I melted into cascading sensations, the aftershocks continuing to squeeze him until I felt his release and watched his satisfaction in the mirror. I loved this man who had redefined my world. We *did* belong together.

CHAPTER 32

He turned me around, holding me, settling us both. "You a little more relaxed now?" he teased.

"Relaxed enough that everything that needs to be done can wait 'til morning." I felt emotional. "It's not just the sex, although that's beyond description," I said, "but there's nothing about you I don't admire. You're an incredible human."

"You make me want to be amazing. I'm not perfect, but when I see me through your eyes, I want to be that man. It almost scares me when I think Edward felt this way, then he was gone. We need to find out what happened to him, Digger. I need to know."

Strange he would be so driven about it, but I'd find out. There had to be records. "We'll find out, Brand, we will."

What an eclectic arrangement of people we had for Thanksgiving. The table was set with a dark green tablecloth covered with a beautiful array of colorful leaves Jeni had collected that morning. The fire was lit, the finest crystal in use, and the wine poured freely.

My father was trying to show displeasure because he knew my returning to New York was a case he couldn't win, but his obvious delight in the characters present was evident. Jeni and her mother, Janet, had long been his favorites, and they continued to be so, even as they dealt with her sweetly clueless grandmother. Miles was a huge help in engaging her Nana.

Janet always looked at the bright side. "Come on, Patricia, in all the time we've known each other, have you ever seen your little girl this happy?"

If she had had one, my mother would have been waving the proverbial fan to calm herself. "But it was so undignified," she said of the termination of my engagement. "To leave everything she had to come here where they don't even have a department store . . . it makes no sense."

Obviously sensing the situation, Sam and Sunni regaled us with wonderful tales of the town, its history, and the people who inhabited it. They told of evenings spent with Billy Joel, John Denver, and many other famous music legends, jamming at the Pioneer Inn during impromptu gatherings.

And the more dinner progressed, the more Brandan and Miles charmed her. After hours of camaraderie, she seemed to glean at least a little understanding of my attraction to the place. "But doesn't Brandan want to live in the City?" she continued to press. "It's so much more civilized."

"There's a lot more we want to accomplish here. Jordan and I won't uproot for a while," Brandan said with confidence.

Silence filled the air as everyone looked at him. There was such an assured degree of future in his statement—*our* future. We looked at each other and I gave a slight nod. "I'll not make any secret of the fact that I want to marry Jordan and have asked her on more than one occasion," he said, looking directly at my father. His gaze drifted to me and a tender smile gentled his rugged features. "One of these days I'm hoping she'll say 'yes.' In the meantime, I'll keep asking," he said, raising his glass as if in a toast.

The table erupted into riotous conversation, everyone giving their opinion of what a perfect union it would be, how beautiful our babies would be, and what was the matter with me that I hadn't said 'yes' immediately? It was a pleasant and wonderful day, and it set the tone for the joy I wanted in this home that we were creating. Even with the varying personalities, the beauty of what was going on here was irresistible.

When the doorbell rang, everyone called in unison, *"COME IN,"* then burst into laughter. April and her young sons and boyfriend came in gingerly, with James Gabriel rushing to throw his arms around me, then Brandan. "I brought you a present, Jordan. Mama showed me a picture, and I made it just like you taught me. Only one little cut on the end of my finger," he said proudly, holding up the digit as he pulled a small item from his pocket with the other hand. It was wrapped in tissue, and while the confusion at the table continued, I took him by the hand to a separate chair so it was just the two of us in a relatively quiet corner.

"I can't wait to see it," I said, unwrapping it carefully as he eagerly helped me tear at the paper. I was moved beyond words when I saw the lopsided turkey that had been carved by his precious hands. "You did this for me?" I asked, having a hard time stemming the tears.

"I worked on it all week," he said proudly. "I thought you'd like it for your table for dinner today, but we just got back from Martin's mom's house," he said, crossing his arms.

"It's all okay now," I said, giving him a hug and kissing him on the forehead. "It's the nicest gift anyone has ever given me."

"Nicest *ever?*" he asked, his eyes getting wide.

"Nicest *ever*," I replied. "Do you want some pie? Brandan is the best pie maker this side of the Mississippi, and you're in for a real treat if you have some room left to eat."

"I love pie. I could eat a whole one all by myself," he said proudly.

"How about a little piece of each one? Does that sound good?"

"Yes, ma'am," he said, taking my hand and leading me back into the enjoyable commotion.

"Will you stay for dessert?" I asked April and Martin. "And Brandan, will you lift James Gabriel so he can set his centerpiece on the Thanksgiving table, please? He carved it all by himself," I announced proudly, going for plates. When I came back, James Gabriel was intense in explaining to my father how I taught him to whittle, just like I used to do when I was his age. Even more special than his explanation was the fact that my father seemed engrossed. Every time I looked his way, my father was laughing.

"You seem to have made a niche for yourself here," Father said after everyone had gone. It was quiet as I cleaned up the kitchen.

"I sure think so."

"Sometimes the events we think are the worst possible incidents that could happen in our lives are the things that bring us the most happiness. I would never have chosen for you to be hurt by Andrew, but look what you got in return."

"I was certainly the winner, wasn't I?"

"Did I mention that I fired Andrew?"

"*What?!* What do you mean? You didn't have to do that!"

"I am well aware of my responsibilities, Jordanna. And I *did* have to do it. Moral integrity is what built Whitman and Burke. If I couldn't trust him with my greatest asset, how could I trust him with the simple ones?"

A whole new appreciation of this complex man overcame me. Putting my arms around him, I rested my head on his chest until I felt him relax in my embrace. "Thank you, Father. I didn't think it mattered, but it does." It was the closest moment we had ever shared. I would treasure it.

"Brandan seems like a good man. You have my approval should you choose to move forward with him."

"That means the world to me, thank you."

I kissed him on the cheek, and we continued to talk as we finished up the kitchen. "Even your mother seems impressed by what you've done around here, although she'd never admit it. Your young James Gabriel stole her heart. It pleased her when you were young that you enjoyed your grandfather's whittling. Neither she nor Madeline ever did. And when you pass the Colorado Bar, maybe we can talk about options for you."

"Not sure what my future looks like right now, but you have my word that when I'm finished with what I'm working on, I'll give it serious consideration."

The holidays passed, and there was no longer work for Brandan around Madeline Manor. He spent many nights with me, and there wasn't a day I didn't appreciate the man he was, the love we shared, and the thrill at what we were finding as I poured through paperwork, did online research, and spent time tracking down history from the local archives.

I was constantly pleased with Joey's initiative. He took care of most of the work around the place and left the enjoyable stuff for me—planning meals, marketing, fixing special meals for guests, and most importantly, giving me time to work on my research.

When the piano was returned, I knew exactly how the first Jordan must have felt with the excitement of its magnificence. It was a work of art, and the most unique instrument I had ever encountered. In what would live in my heart as one of my greatest discoveries, Brandan would sometimes play touchingly haunting tunes, and I could almost hear the music that lingered in this home where Edward and his Jordan has shared such love.

Edward's journal stopped abruptly when Jordan was six months pregnant, and county records showed a marriage license issued two months later to a Jordan Stratton and Andrew Harriman. I felt as though I had lost a dear friend, and felt somehow betrayed by Jordan. What could have happened to have caused such a change in fate, and how could she have loved Edward as much as she did and then marry someone else so soon after his death? I was heartsick over this turn of events.

"Listen, Digger," Brandan said one night as I was stepping out of the shower. "It's less than a month before the invited relatives arrive. Maybe some of them will have answers?"

"Maybe," I said. "I just can't find anything that would explain why she would have married so soon, or what happened to Edward. His death certificate said 'internal bleeding,' but what caused it, *who* caused it, and how *could* she? If something happened to you, I could never think of being with someone else."

He squeezed me. "It was different then. She was pregnant and widowed. It had to have been difficult for a woman alone in 1894 under those circumstances, in what must have been the middle of nowhere. This place was deserted. The silver and tungsten mines were closing, people were moving back to Denver, I can't conceive how lonely it must've been for her."

"I know, you're right. She didn't have family around, there wasn't electricity or phones, no cars, harsh winters. Okay, I'll cut her some slack, but what happened?"

"You'll find out," he said, kissing me. I loved learning what a sensual experience kissing could be as he got harder. He set me on the counter, my legs around his hips, my arms around his neck, sharing a deep kiss, mentally seeing myself being absorbed into him. I was on the edge of the granite, hot and wet when his finger found me.

His tongue on my lips moved in the same pattern as his finger – hard then soft against me, circling, thrusting, teasing, making my juices flow in anticipation. I wanted him completely. It was such an intense experience I wondered if I could find fulfillment with just our dueling tongues. I leaned back and propped myself on my elbows, exposing myself to him. I was desperate, ready as I raised my hips to meet him thrust for thrust. When I opened my eyes and saw him watching me, I wanted him— possessing me.

He brought my arms around his neck. His strength was impressive as he raised me then lowered me onto his shaft, driving into me. I was partially balanced on the counter, partially being supported by him, and the angle was hitting all the right places. The rhythm of his hips and watching the play of muscle across his chest from the strength of his arms supporting me brought me over the edge, and when we climaxed together, I was clinging and holding on so tightly I knew I would leave marks.

I'm not sure when it happened, but something in my heart had changed. There was no going back. He carried me to the bed, and I fell asleep wrapped up with him, content to my soul. Sometime in the middle of the night, I came awake as though someone had tapped me on my shoulder.

"Brandan! Wake up!" I said.

He smiled about the same time one eye opened to look up at me. "It had better be good to have disturbed that awesome dream I was having."

"That wasn't a dream, silly, that was how you went to sleep last night. But listen, listen, how in the world did we forget?! We put a duffel bag back in the secret room in the trunk. I haven't thought of it since I got back and the bathroom was built around it! Maybe there's something there!"

CHAPTER 33

I was unconcerned with my naked state as I ran to the bathroom and opened the secret door. Brandan came in leisurely and put my robe around me. "It's 28 degrees. You may want this."

"How can you be so practical at a time like this? It may all be in here!" I was energized.

"And it may not be. Don't get too far ahead of yourself."

I was frustrated with the locks on the duffel bag and turned to hand it to him. "Please make it work," I said, half teasing, half desperate.

We ended up in the kitchen with Brandan's trusty set of tools. After a few minutes, he had both locks open. "Be my guest," he said, touching my cheek and leaning over to hug me as he handed the bag to me. "You're welcome to bring it upstairs if you'd like. It won't disturb me. I sleep better when you're around, awake or asleep."

I wanted to tear into the bag, dump the contents on the table and see what was there. "Okay, I'll give you the one extra minute it takes to race you to the bed," I said with a laugh, tearing off up the stairs. He wasn't immediately behind me, but when he came in the room he said, "Someone had to turn out the lights on the way up. I hope there never comes a time when your racing doesn't make me laugh."

I was on the bed, looking at him expectantly. "I waited, but I can't wait any more. I can't even believe I forgot this was in there. I hope I'm not horribly disappointed." He sat down next to me, squeezed me, then gave me space.

"Okay, open it up. Unless there's gold in there, I'm going to sleep while you filter through the contents."

I didn't make a sound. Brandan opened one eye, then sat up next to me. "What is it, sweetheart?"

"It's all letters from Jordan. Most of them are to Willow! It's better than every Christmas present put together! It may take me weeks to read them all, but can you imagine what's in them? Oh, my God! Oh, my God!"

He relaxed again, laying his head on the pillow. "I'm here if you need me," he said with a yawn.

Carefully I opened the first letter, wondering about the woman who had written it over a hundred years ago, about the people who might have read it since.

Dear Willow: As long as I live I will spend my life making up to you the wrongs I have caused. My prayer is that now that the cottage is finished, you and I will be able to stay here in peace, me with my painting and quilting, you as you grow into a beautiful young woman despite your step-father's cruelty. I thought he would get over it in time, but the sight of you is a constant reminder of my dearest love. I never professed to love your step-father. Nothing will ever replace what I felt for Edward, and I never thought to keep that a secret. Maybe I should have, but it would deny my very being. There is not a day that Edward does not walk beside me. I have been a good wife to Andrew and have no guilt. What I felt for Edward comes along only once in a lifetime. I pray you will find someone in your life who means as much to you.

This was the beginning of dozens if not scores of letters. I held my breath as I opened the next one.

The world is changing rapidly, Willow. Your sister Adelaine has a sweet spirit, but your heart and your intelligence are exceptional, and you remind me often of your father, even your mannerisms. It grieves me to say this about my own son, but at the age of seven, I see daily he is his father's son. He has the same devious nature as his sire, and I have not been able to love it out of him, nor to separate him long enough from Andrew to have had a chance of changing his very nature. Andrew takes such pride in making our son into his image, a replica I find abhorrent. If I thought there was a way to escape and change him, I would take all of you and run, but I surmise the damage was done at birth. He is well and truly Andrew's son, and sometimes I fear him, this child of my womb.

T.R. Roosevelt, a man I have long admired, is President. Your father used to tease me about my affection for the young T.R. who loved his wife Alice almost as much as your father loved me. I was not much older than you, dear Willow, when I first read how T.R. was almost destroyed when his young bride died at the age of 22, two days after the birth of their daughter Alice. To make it even more tragic, his mother, to whom he was close, also died on the same day, Valentine's day, four years to the day after his engagement to Alice. My tender heart bled for him when I read about the double funeral, and then leaving the baby Alice with his sister and going to the Dakotas on a 'personal discovery journey.'

He would never speak again of 'his heart's dearest dying, and the light leaving his life forever,' not even to his daughter who would ask often about her mother. Her aunt was the one who told her stories of her mother, never her father. He remarried, of course, as I understand so well how that can happen, but I often empathize with his plight. There is not a day that passes that I don't love your father and wish for what might have been. I pray good things for our country as you grow and T.R. implements his progressive ideas and plans into action. But unlike T.R., I want you to know everything I can remember about your father so his memory lives on in you and in your children.

Your step-father has invested more money, this time in a town some distance away called Las Vegas. He and some friends have purchased land there. I pray to God he will stay and leave us in peace, and, God forgive me, keep your half brother with him. Daily I wonder how I could have married Andrew. Your father hated him so.

Before I married your father, I was engaged to Andrew. Edward always said how glad he was that I found out about Andrew's cheating ways and broke off our engagement. Some day I will tell you how I came to marry him, but it is a decision I have daily regretted.

Follow your heart, Willow, no matter what. Trust your gut. It's there, my darling, to protect you. Do not second guess yourself. No matter how much you analyze something, what you believe at first almost always turns out to be truth. Trust yourself. You are so smart and such a light. I know you will change the world in ways I can't even imagine. Your father would be so proud of you.

Rather than feeling like I had learned something, I felt there were so many more unanswered questions. The thrill of my find would keep me awake for days.

Andrew and Adler left last week for Nevada. The men believe they can make a great town out of this new place called Las Vegas. My heart rejoices at the freedom you and Adelaine and I will have during this time. We are going into Spring, and they will not return before winter. I wonder what kind of a black heart I must have to pray they will not come back. Maybe life will be so different and gay for them that they realize how dreary it is in Nederland with so many having left town.

I read letter after letter before I finally set them aside and curled into Brandan's side. He instinctively cocooned me. I had new insight, with some understanding of how Jordan's mind worked. I was wonderfully glad that neither Brandan nor I came from Adler's lineage, although I was still angry that I was a progeny of Andrew.

It was ten a.m. when I woke. There was a note on the side table from Brandan that he hadn't wanted to wake me, but he looked forward to finding out what I had discovered in the night. I took a hot shower and made some coffee to clear my foggy brain. I had a date with a hundred year old story.

CHAPTER 34

Do you love our evenings as much as I do, Willow? They are peaceful by the fire as I teach Adelaine to quilt while you play the piano. You have such a natural talent with a voice that would surely delight the angels. Your father loved when I would play for him. In the mornings now I sometimes play for hours, hoping somehow he can hear me. It's when I feel closest to him. There are not many hours I don't miss him.

It warmed my heart that Jordan loved Willow as much as she did. I couldn't help but hope she had spoken these feelings aloud as well.

If he had been standing in front of me, I would have shot him between the eyes without one ounce of regret or a moment's warning.

So began the fourth letter of the morning. It was obvious from her writing she had found Edward's journal. Tragic it had taken a dozen years to do so. It must have been heartbreaking to read his tender words of love not only to her, but to their soon-to-be-born child.

Oh, Edward, what have I done? You tried to warn me, but I thought you were being wonderfully jealous. Did Andrew have something to do with your death as you suspected? Was I so distraught that I couldn't see reality around me? If it hadn't been for Willow, I would not have lived. All I wanted was to die with you, so great was my pain. But our child lived in me, and I would do nothing to stop your blood from flowing through her. I will visit Mr. Witherspoon at the Land Office and find if there is truth to Andrew's involvement. I will ruin them if I find that is the case. Nothing will stop me.

There were two weeks between that letter and the next. *Dearest Willow: I am entrusting this letter with my cousin. If anything happens to me, she has been instructed to give you this missive.*

Andrew was responsible for the murder of your father. I will never forgive myself for being so blind, but I will make him pay for it. I went to see Mr. Witherspoon. I tried to find him for weeks, but no one knew of his whereabouts. I finally paid a visit to his home where I found him dying of consumption. He would tell me nothing. I felt no shame in slapping him several times. When he realized I would kill him quicker than the tuberculosis from which he suffered, he offered me his deathbed confession.

My dearest Edward struck gold. In wanting to protect me and the child I carried, he spirited away nuggets, but was afraid Andrew (whom he often called Simon Legree) had discovered his secret. Not wanting to put me at risk, he left early one morning to see Mr. Witherspoon and file his claim before someone else could strong-arm him out of it. According to the ailing Mr. Witherspoon, he and Andrew struck a deal after your father left. In exchange for a third of whatever treasures were found at the vein, Mr. Witherspoon would put Andrew's name on as the lien holder instead of Edward's. It was a terrible wrong, one they knew Edward would fight.

They made arrangements with an outlaw who was passing through town. In exchange for his run-away horse knocking Edward down as he crossed the street, this man would stop at Mr. Witherspoon's on his way out of town and collect the second half of his payment for killing your father. Two hundred dollars in exchange for the life of one of the finest men who ever lived.

I have relived that moment hundreds of times. Me heavy with child, and Andrew coming to console me that Edward had been killed when a horse crushed him. Nothing made sense in my life any more. Andrew was so solicitous and offered me anything money could buy. And to think it was Edward's money he was using, I have even more desire to kill him.

I will return to Mr. Witherspoon's tomorrow to make him sign a confession. I will take the Sheriff with me to have as a witness. Andrew will not get away with this any longer.

I was shaking as I finished reading this letter. I hated Andrew.

CHAPTER 35

The big weekend had finally arrived, and I was looking forward to meeting everyone. Not only were we about to meet long-lost relatives, but the thought of them shedding light on more of the family's history was exciting. The doorbell rang, and Brandan was already speaking to the thin, tall man when I came down the stairs.

"Jordan, this is Austin Bridgewater from St. Louis. Austin, Jordan Whitman, owner of Madeline Manor and your hostess for the weekend."

I disliked him on sight and hoped the others would not strike me so repulsively. With barely a nod, he walked over to take a closer look at the piano. Brandan and I exchanged a look that spoke volumes, but I wanted to at least make an effort. "I'm so pleased you were able to join us, Austin. Do you have family with you?"

Ignoring my question, he said, "There's been a lot of oral history passed down through my family about this house, but no actual records. Sometime along the way it became known as 'the big house in the mountains,' but no one even knew what city it was in. Imagine my surprise when I received the note of your inheritance," he said with what sounded like a whine. "It's in pristine condition," he added, looking around.

"It's taken hundreds of hours of hard work to get it to this condition. Brandan and his crew worked for many months to make it resemble its previous glory," I smiled, trying to be pleasant to this person that made every part of my spirit hiss. "Which line of the family are you from?"

"I am the grandson of Augusta and Cranston Bridgewater, and the son of Joan and Avery Bridgewater."

Please, God, let the others arriving be more pleasant, I prayed. What a thoroughly unpleasant man. I was trying to remember names and where they fit, but I had a detailed family tree upstairs and would check it shortly. "You're the first guest to arrive. Let me show you to your room."

"I'll take him, Jordan," Brandan offered. "Is Austin in The Gables?"

"Yes, thank you. I'll check on dinner, if you'll excuse me, Austin?" I asked in the most syrupy voice I could muster. He followed Brandan as though I had never spoken. If this was a sign of things to come, it was going to be a long weekend.

With each arriving guest, I grew more hopeful for the days ahead. All but Austin seemed delighted to be here and to share information. Dinner was a spirited affair with Joey helping with serving and cleaning which allowed me time to sit with guests, collect information, and hear new stories that filled in missing some pieces. It was an energetic and exciting time—except for Austin. Every time I saw him, I went cold. How could he be related to this wonderful group of people?

He offered nothing throughout the evening. When asked questions, he would reply with a bored expression and nothing more than 'yes' or 'no' responses. At some point he asked, "When you were doing the remodeling, did you happen to find anything interesting?"

"You'd have to ask Brandan," I offered, wondering what he could possibly be getting at. "Brandan was in on the day-to-day demolition. I was just the one who stood on the sidelines and cracked the whip."

That brought laughter from those assembled, except, of course, Austin. But I would never reveal what we found in the letters. I would share some of the photos, but Edward's journal and Jordan's letters to Willow were private. We were still looking for answers.

There were eighteen people present. Joey graciously stayed with a friend so four people could stay in his quarters. The house was bursting with people and laughter. It was no surprise that Austin was the only one who brought nothing with him by way of letters or photos. Several times I caught him looking in closets, opening doors he had no business opening, and generally making my skin crawl.

At one point in the evening he walked out. When he was gone about fifteen minutes, I excused myself and went looking for him. He was coming down the back staircase that led to my office. "Can I help you find something?" I asked, more pleasant than I felt. "Were you looking for something in particular?"

"No," was his response as he passed me, entered his room and closed the door. I immediately looked to see if anything had been disturbed. A drawer was partially open, but since we kept nothing in here that could be compromised if it had been found, it served to put me more on alert. What could he possibly be looking for?

The rest of us stayed up for hours passing along oral family history and sharing pictures and letters that had been passed down through their families. There were obviously more from the most recent generations, but the ones from three and four generations back, while not many, were fascinating, especially to Brandan and me. Throughout the evening I thought how beguiling it was that Brandan was not only enjoying this, but these were *his* relatives as well.

In a bond that had been formed a century and a quarter beforehand, he felt like my destiny. The more I was with him, the more I knew I didn't want to live without him. When the weekend was over, I would accept the marriage proposal he offered regularly. I couldn't bear the thought of not having him in my life.

We had interesting outings and meals planned after late morning tomorrow, and everyone retired for the evening sated from wine, fine food, and wonderful conversation. I was thrilled with the gathering. Blowing out candles, Brandan and I stood in the darkened dining room wrapped in each other's arms. "I'm so proud of you," he said, resting his chin on my head and folding me in his arms. "We couldn't have asked for a better interchange or group of people. It was a brilliant idea, Digger. I'm looking forward to gathering all of these pieces and seeing how they fit together."

"Yes," I said under my breath, "everyone except Austin. What a strange duck he is."

"Good to hear. I disliked him on sight, but no idea why."

"I'm so glad. I found him prowling around in the office, but he came down as though he had every right to be there. He was looking for something."

"I'll be sure to keep an eye on him tomorrow. In the meantime, let's go take a look at your family tree. I want to know where the hell he came from."

He looked around to make sure everything was turned off, winked at me, and took off in a run. Not expecting this playfulness from him at this time of night, he easily beat me to Willow Tree. We turned on only the tiny lights that surrounded the bed as I pulled out the separate pieces of paper we had previously graphed. There were so many branches and lost lines that it was hard to keep track of everyone's direct lineage, but it would be fun tomorrow to share these pages at brunch and have everyone fill in what they might know that I had not have been able to find. But for now, all I was interested in was Austin.

"How could we not have known?" I whispered a few minutes later as I traced him back five generations. "I knew I hated him on sight, so I should have guessed."

"What—tell me," Brandan asked, coming in from the bathroom and making sure the connecting door was closed before he sat down.

"He's Andrew's great-great-grandson," I said, still speaking softly, as though I didn't want anyone to know we were harboring the spawn of satan in our home. "Andrew and Jordan Harriman had their wretched son Adler. They appear to have kept the 'A' names going through the generations. Adler married a woman named Jenna who died during childbirth when their daughter Ada was born. Adler then married a woman named Rose who had a daughter from a previous marriage named Mary Beth, then Adler and Rose had a daughter named Augusta. So Adler, the evil son of Jordan, had two of his own daughters, Ada and Augusta, and a step-daughter named Mary Beth.

"Augusta married Cranston Bridgewater. Their second son was Avery, who married Joan, who spawned Austin. Austin appears to have no siblings, thank God," I smiled, looking over at Brandan. "Did any of that make sense?"

"The easiest thing to follow was that Austin is a direct descendant of Andrew's son Adler. That's all I need to know to make sure we keep a close eye on him while he's here. Not sure he can do much damage, but I'm not predisposed to give him the benefit of the doubt," he said. "The guy's a creep and I don't even know him. And what he *did* tell us, I don't believe for a minute. I'll be vigilant."

"Thank you," I said, putting my hand on his. "I don't know what it is about him, but I agree. I wish I could ask him to leave in the morning. I'll keep an eye out too. Between the two of us, we should be able to keep a snake in a cage, right?"

I fell asleep the way I wanted to fall asleep for the rest of my days, in Brandan's arms. Sometime in the night, a noise woke us, and we threw on our clothes and tip-toed to the kitchen. Austin was standing in the middle of the kitchen with a flashlight when Brandan flipped on the light. "Are you looking for something?" Brandan asked casually. Austin didn't even look phased when he said, "I was hoping to find a snack."

Brandan and I exchanged a look of 'yeah, right,' but I politely offered to make him something to eat as there were lots of leftovers. "No. I'll pass. I'm no longer hungry," he said as he walked past us.

"Grrrr, I can't stand him," I said quietly. "What nerve."

"Indeed. When I offered to be vigilant, I didn't think that meant through the middle of the night."

"Come on back to bed. It's not like there's anything in the house he would be able to find. Anything of value is in Willow Tree, right?"

"I agree, but I can't help but wonder what he's looking for."

CHAPTER 36

The day dawned crisp and clear. I had a special brunch planned for everyone, then sack lunches for those who might want to go exploring. Anyone who wanted could stay and share family stories, or just get to know each other. It was a wonderful time.

When Austin hadn't come down by the time brunch was finished, I asked Brandan to check on him. He didn't answer the knock and the door was locked. Cornering me in the kitchen, he said, "Privacy be damned, I want to open the door. I don't think he's in there." I told him I didn't have a problem with him unlocking the door in the guise of safety for our guest, and sure enough, the room was empty. Doing a cursory glance around the room, we relocked the door and rejoined our guests.

Sam came to the back door about an hour later and asked me to step outside with him. Brandan joined us as Sam recounted how Austin was asking questions around town that were putting people on edge. "Don't wanna cause no trouble, mind ya, but he's been askin' 'bout gold. Wantin' to know if anyone ever heard rumors 'bout there bein' any kinda buried treasure round here. Course ain't nobody gonna tell him a derned thing, but I thought ya outta know. He gives me the creeps, and I had ta hold Sunni back from spittin' on the varmit," he chuckled.

I hugged Sam and said, "You've got some good radar, my friend, and we're thankful you came and told us. Any idea where he is now?"

"He left the Pioneer Inn 'bout an hour ago and I ain't heard nothin' since. But ya best believe we're all on the lookout."

"Thank you so much. I'm not sure what it all means, but it's good information. We'll be on guard. Oh! Before you go, hold on." I grabbed a couple of bags. "You took such good care of me. I know it's not much, but here's some special fixings I made for lunches today. There's one for you and Sunni. Figure you gotta get tired of eating your own cooking," I teased.

"Aw, get on with ya now. Sunni'll be a might thankful," he chuckled.

"What in the world do you suppose *that* is about?" I asked as we stood watching Sam drive away. "Gold? For real?"

"Makes you wonder what the oral family history was, doesn't it? And they didn't even know what town we were in, only 'the big house in the mountains.' Interesting."

By the time Austin arrived home, it was late evening and everyone was heading to bed. No one said anything, but it was clear they were giving him plenty of room as they continued on their way. No one had asked about him today.

"Where'd you spend *your* day?" Brandan asked as the last guest left the living room.

"In Boulder. Doing research."

"What kind of research?" I asked.

"Going through public records in the library," he said, looking at his fingernails as though something distasteful might have touched them.

"Looking for anything in particular?" I asked, thinking I sounded defensive.

"Trying to find out how you came to inherit this place since it was owned by my great-great-grandfather."

I felt my blood pressure immediately skyrocket. "How dare you?" I hissed.

Brandan put his arm around me to calm me and give me his strength. I was about to let loose when Brandan said quietly, "It was indirectly in your family, but it was deeded to Adelaine Harriman McGinnis, Jordan's great-grandmother, and not to your great-grandfather Adler. The house has never been in your family line."

"We'll see about that," he said as though we were talking of the weather. Good Lord, this man made me sick to my stomach.

"You are a most unpleasant man, Austin, just like your ancestors before you." I could see Brandan's smile from the corner of my eye. "I would appreciate it if you would leave in the morning. You are not even welcome to join us for breakfast. As a matter of fact, I have no wish you see you again, so please remove yourself from these premises at your earliest convenience." I appeared composed as I walked up the stairs.

"You heard the lady," Brandan said. "You've overstayed your welcome. I expect you to be gone by sunrise."

I was pacing by the time Brandan made it to our room. "I've never . . . I'm so *angry* . . . of all the *nerve* . . ."

"You're sputtering," he teased, taking me in his arms. "You're right about all of it. He'll be gone in the morning. I'll see to it personally."

"What gall! What a *jerk!* Arrgghhh, I'm not sure I've ever disliked anyone so much in my life."

"We've hated Andrew as long as we've known about him. No surprise we would hate his offspring as well."

"What would I do without you?" I asked, pulling him tightly to me. "I'd be going to jail tonight, that's what.

I'd kill him with my bare hands. I'd slice him into pieces." I invented ways to take that bored, self-satisfied smirk off his face.

"Who knew you were such a little hell-cat?" he grinned. "This is a side of you I haven't seen before, but I *like* it! Wanna take some of your energy out on me?" he asked, lifting my chin and kissing me. The gentleness of his kiss set me on fire. I pulled his shirt off in record time and had him undressed and flat on his back on the bed.

What followed was unbelievably passionate lovemaking. I did things to him I'd never dreamed of, and wouldn't let him take the lead. This was *my* release, *my* fantasy, and I loved every minute of it. Obviously he did too.

"How did you do that?" I panted. "How did a gentle kiss ignite that kind of response?"

"I don't know, but I'll have to remember it," he said, cradling my head against his shoulder as we both fell exhausted into a blissful sleep.

Sometime early in the morning, I felt him crawling back into bed. "He's gone," he said quietly. "His room is cleared out and his car is gone."

"Thank God. I've loved everyone who came here but him," I said sleepily. "We have another hour or so. Can you sleep?"

"I'm sure I can," he said, pulling me against him, "as long as you're here." He was asleep by the third breath. I would tell him my decision when everyone was gone. I rested peacefully in his arms until the alarm went off.

"They'll all be gone by noon," I said as I was leaving the room. "Let's plan on spending some quiet time together. Joey and his friend want to earn extra money, so they're gonna take care of the mess from a full house. Maybe you and I can do a picnic?"

"I know just the place," he smiled. "It'll be fun. Even as enjoyable as it's been, it's been a long few days."

"Yeah, but there've been some nice interludes," I wisecracked, remembering last night. "I'll meet you downstairs."

The hugs and excitement from departing guests lasted most of the morning. I had taken photos of their photos, and now my job was to compile the information we'd collected and put it into a neat package on a disc they would each receive. Brandan and I had already discussed how much of Edward and Jordan's information would be released. Brandan had driven a group to the airport in Denver and was expected back soon. I was outside waving to the last of the guests when I heard a 'pssssst' coming from the direction of the cottage. Stepping off the porch, I heard it again.

"Jordan, over here." It was James Gabriel, hiding behind a tree.

"What are you doing back here, honey?" I asked quietly, looking around to see why he was being secretive.

"That man is sneaking around," he whispered.

"What man do you mean?" I asked, but my skin crawled knowing exactly who he was talking about.

"The man that was in town yesterday that nobody liked. I was with Mama and heard her talking to somebody, them telling her not to say a word to him. Then she tells me not to go near him. I didn't, but he's been in the woods this morning. Brandan left and that guy was at the cottage. I just seen him go in your back door," he said it so quietly I had to strain to hear him.

"You've done a wonderful job, little man. Now I need to you listen to me carefully, okay? I need you to run home," I said, looking around. "You tell your Mama to call Brandan and Miles and tell them what you just told me. Okay? Tell them both to get back here as soon as they can. Then make sure she calls the police. Do you understand?" He nodded solemnly, holding up his little finger. "Pinky swear I'll do exactly like you told me," he said.

After we released pinkies, I hugged him then turned him toward home. "Hurry, darling. And don't slow down for anyone."

CHAPTER 37

I came in the back door quietly. There were no sounds except the whirring of the refrigerator motor. Where was Joey? And where was Austin? I was now beginning to think as Edward had—Simon Legree. Silently I searched the first and second floor, knife in hand, listening between footfalls. No sound, no movement.

Taking each step one tread at a time, I could hear noise as I opened the office door, but he wasn't there. I listened carefully, but my pounding pulse drowned out what I thought I heard. As my heart rate slowed, the sound was coming from the other side of the wall, but was it in the bathroom or my room? I didn't want to open the secret passages to give away the disguise, so I retraced my steps to the stairs that led to Willow Tree.

Inch by slow inch so as to make no sound, I worked my way to my room. I could hear rummaging, could hear drawers being opened and closed, and could hear what could only be described as destruction. I feared he would find the pass-through at any moment, and moved a little faster to interrupt his tirade.

"Looking for something?" I asked, leaning nonchalantly against the door jamb. There were clothes strewn everywhere. My heart rate would have given away my indifference, but on the outside I looked serene.

"Where is it?" he asked with a sneer.

"What are you talking about?" I marveled at how this indifferent, non-reactionary man was now snarling like an animal. "I don't have a clue what you're looking for."

"Don't be coy with me. Everyone knows the first owner hid gold in the house. You just finished reconstruction. You have to have found it."

"Oh, poor Austin. You just got yourself into a whole lotta trouble for nothing. There was no gold. Your greed has gained you absolutely nothing."

I was trying to push him to the brink. I wanted to cut his heart out for what his ancestor had done to Edward, to Jordan, to Willow. I wanted to make him pay for all the heartache Andrew had caused. Pushing away from the wall, I was aware my lines between then and now had blurred, that it was not reasonable or rational that he could or should pay for their sins, but I could make him pay for his own. The apple hadn't fallen far from the tree. Austin was every bit as evil and black-hearted as his predecessors.

"Game's up," I said, stepping into the room and clearing the doorway. I crossed my arms over my chest with the knife showing. "Walk on down the stairs, Austin. By the time we get to the bottom, the police should be here. There's no gold, but there will be charges."

"Seriously? You presume I'm afraid of you?" he asked, pulling the gun from his waistband. "If you think I'm going back to jail, you're sadly mistaken. Your lover's in Denver, and it's just you and me to decide who will be the victor. I'll trust my gun over your knife."

I knew I could have the gun out of his hand in three seconds flat, but I needed to make sure I was in position. "This is how it's going to be," he said with disdain in a look I expected was just like Andrew. "You're going down the stairs in front of me. Then I'm going to take you as far as my car and drive away—

alone. Unless you piss me off even more. Then I'll leave your body on the side of the road and not look back."

"I wish you hadn't said that," Brandan said from the doorway. Shocked, both Austin and I turned to the voice that commanded attention with its silent menace. Leveling the barrel of his gun directly at my head, Austin said, "Get out of my way or I'll shoot." Brandan and I looked at each other, but his presence complicated what should have been an easy situation. I knew my ability, but now Austin seemed even more crazed. He pulled the hammer on the gun and said, "One . . . Two . . ."

Brandan leapt for Austin at the exact moment I released my knife. It found its mark in the side of Austin's neck exactly where I had intended—to maim, not kill. The explosion of the handgun was deafening as Austin was dropped by the blow of the blade. In what felt like slow motion, Brandan was hurtled backward by the impact of the bullet. The scream sounded like my voice, but I didn't know how to stop it. Brandan lay lifeless on the floor, bleeding from a massive chest wound. What had I done? Oh, God, what had I done?!

I flung myself over him, checking frantically to see if he was breathing. No movement, no breath from his lips. I cradled his head against my chest, sobbing, crying out to God to spare his life. I grabbed a shirt from the floor, pressing it into the wound to stem the flow of blood that pulsed profusely from his chest. Miles was there, taking me by the shoulders. *"NO!"* I screamed. *"He can't be dead!"*

Miles held onto my blood-covered body while a policeman tried to stop the hemorrhaging. Within minutes there were paramedics, hooking him to IVs, carrying him out on a stretcher, all the while, blood seeping. "What have I done, Miles? What have I done?!" I cried, holding on to him. "Miles, tell me he's going to live."

"Stop it, Jordan, you didn't do this! You didn't pull the trigger. You were protecting yourself. *You didn't do this!*"

"I invited that serpent into our home, Miles. It's all my fault."

There were a dozen people in the crowded room. Austin lay bleeding on the floor, motionless, while someone knelt next to him, more appearing to be choking him rather than trying to stop the blood flow. "I need to go with him, Miles. I need to be there."

He followed me to the ambulance. Uncaring of anything, I slipped into the back. They were working on him, monitoring him. I had to be in control, had to be silent and unobserved or they'd make me leave. The sirens wailed as we wound through Boulder Canyon. The blood was not coming so fast now. He was breathing. I wanted to ask if he would live, but didn't want to draw attention from whatever they were doing to help him.

When we arrived at Boulder Memorial Hospital there was a team of doctors and nurses waiting. They rushed him to Emergency, but blocked me from entering. "Please," I begged, "please let me be with him."

"You may wait in the waiting room, Mrs. Webb. We'll come get you when he's stabilized." I didn't want to volunteer the information that I wasn't his wife. What if they wouldn't let me see him?

Someone brought me a blanket. At some point they brought me water. I was numb to everything until Miles was sitting next to me, holding me, rocking me. "Please tell me he's going to live. Tell me something."

"They'll be out soon, then we'll have a better idea. Of course he's going to live, silly, he's Brandan."

"The blood. How could there have been so much blood? I'll gladly offer some of mine for a transfusion.

I'll do anything I can to take back those few seconds. Please, dear God, I need him more than You do," I prayed.

Someone came and told us he was being taken to surgery, they'd let us know as soon as he was out. That was hours ago. Why were they taking so long? Where was he? I needed to see him. Needed to tell him it was my fault, tell him how sorry I was, that I never should have thrown the knife.

Someone was shaking my shoulder. The sun was up. "Mrs. Webb, wake up. Mrs. Webb, he's out of surgery."

"He's alive?!"

"He's in a coma. The next forty-eight hours will be critical, but we have him stabilized if you'd like to come back for just a few minutes. He's in intensive care, so you can't stay long."

I almost collapsed when I saw him. How could I not have told him how much I loved him? How could I not have told him I'd marry him? He had loved me so unconditionally and now I was the cause of him being here. "Brandan," I whispered to his lifeless body. "Brandan, I love you so much. You're the strongest person I've ever met. You have to fight, for me, for us. I don't want to live without you now that I've found you. Please, Brandan, I need you to trust me one more time."

Nothing. No change in the drug-induced slow heart rate. No change in his breathing. I kissed his forehead but the nurse came and touched my arm. "You need to leave now, Mrs. Webb. Why don't you go home and clean up? He'll be right here when you get back."

Rather than reassuring me, her words frightened me. Someone led me to the room where Miles was waiting. "Come on, Jordan, let's get you into some fresh clothes. I just talked to Joey and they've released the crime scene. We'll come back in a bit. It won't do Brandan any good if you get sick."

I let out a sob when I thought of Willow Tree as a crime scene, history repeating itself, Edward and Andrew's descendants in conflict after all this time.

"Joey and his friend cleaned up so you don't have to face that."

Nothing was out of place. It looked as though nothing had ever been disturbed.

"Shall I wait while you get cleaned up?"

"No, I may rest for a bit. It's hard to breathe," I said choking.

"I'm not leaving. I'll be here," he said.

"Miles!" I called.

"Yes?" he asked at the doorway.

"Thank you."

"Of course," he said, almost out the door.

"Miles!" I called again.

"Yes?" he said with a smile.

"I forgot to ask. I don't care whether he's alive or not, but what happened to Simon?"

"Who?" he asked.

"I meant Austin. What happened to Austin?"

"He's going to live, but when he gets out he'll be charged with attempted murder."

"Maybe he won't be charged," I said in a monotone. "I may finish the job and kill him before he gets out. Save everyone the trouble."

"Stand in line."

CHAPTER 38

I kept pulling the door open to the hidden room, wondering if there were secrets still undiscovered, wondering if the oral tradition from Austin's family could have been true. Would Edward have mentioned it? Even if he had, those entries or letters could have been lost for a hundred years.

This was a nightmare, and all I wanted was to wake up. I was clean, but there was no way I would be able to sleep here yet. I found Miles in the kitchen with Joey and Kent. "I'll never be able to repay you, I couldn't have faced it," I said.

"Yeah, it was pretty gruesome. But you go sit with Brandan, we'll hold down the fort here. You do your job, I'll do mine," he said affectionately.

Miles put his arm around me and said, "It's gonna be all right, let's go see how the patient's doing."

The drive took forever. There was no change in Brandan's condition. I sat with him, held his hand, poured my heart out. They'd make me leave again. Miles and I sat in the waiting room for hours. Jack came by several times, offering comfort. I didn't miss an opportunity when I went in to tell Brandan all the things I hadn't told him before.

Our emotional fears seem silly at times like this. I'd been afraid of commitment because I'd been hurt and questioned my decision making. How could I trust myself when I'd made such a colossal blunder before? I'd change all that now. I'd let him know how much I loved him without reservation, I'd not stop telling him how much I appreciate him, how much I appreciate all he does for me, how much I love how he loves me.

Three times they allowed me in for short periods, three times I ran my fingers through his hair, whispering in his ear, telling him my heart. I begged him to fight, sharing that if he left me I'd spend the rest of my life in jail. "You can't let Andrew's descendant succeed. Do you hear me? I'll kill Austin with my bare hands."

I had Miles take me home at sunset. The house was spotless. Joey had gone above and beyond.

Something nagged at me but remained elusive. I wandered through each room, holding myself together, not flying into pieces. Brandan was everywhere, just as I imagine Edward was for Jordan after his death. I kept thinking of her, thinking what it must have been like in 1894 to be seven months pregnant in the middle of nowhere, the man you adore has been killed, you're alone.

Andrew would be solicitous. He vows to take care of you, vows not to make demands on you, tells you he understands your loss, but his true character is hidden because your pain is acute. I could never have done it, but I could see how even a strong woman like the pregnant Jordan could have chosen that alternative a century ago. How bereft she must have been coming back here, not hearing his voice, no electricity, no running water, a baby on the way. It had to have been devastating.

Fatigue overtook me. I turned on one row of lights and stood—remembering. I kept thinking of Edward and Jordan. Where did she sleep? What was she thinking? And Edward, he had done so much to take care of her, to provide for her, to warn her, to protect her. I couldn't sleep in here, but I was so tired. I went down to my old room, what was now The Big Apple, and fell asleep seeing them, feeling their passion, knowing and understanding her heartbreak, dreaming of what it must have been like.

I came awake with a start. I needed to know how Brandan was. I called the hospital, no change. I paced. What was the dream that remained elusive? I pulled one of the flashlights out of the drawer to head downstairs, hoping something would register, all the while thinking Edward would have provided for Jordan knowing he was in danger.

I was in the kitchen boiling water for tea when it struck me. I *knew* he would have provided for her and Willow, he would have wanted them taken care of. Turning off the water and taking the stairs two at a time, I opened the connecting door through the bookcase into the bathroom, trying to mentally trace Edward's steps, trying to get into Edward's brain, trying to figure out where he might have hidden something. It had to be in here, he'd taken too much time and effort to make this room, to hide it from even the most observant. But Jordan had found it, and her journal and letters were here, along with Edward's. Who had put them all here? Had it been Willow?

I opened the secret door to the trunk room. Was there something in the chest we hadn't found? It was so dark in here, I'd bring it into the light of day. It didn't budge when I pulled. I lifted the lid and shined the flashlight inside, but it was empty. Much as I had done with the bookcase all those months ago, I sat on the ground and tried to use the strength of my legs to push it. It gave a fraction of an inch. It wasn't adhered to the ground.

Nothing held it there but its own weight. *Its weight!* It was so heavy! I looked inside again, but there was nothing. It was thick oak, but there was no way it could have weighed that much. I kept pressing on the floor of the trunk. There was slight movement, and then I knew.

Frantically I used my arm to measure. The bottom of the trunk was at least six inches lower than the floor of the trunk. Oh, Brandan, how I wanted him here! He would know what to do. I kept picturing the shelf latch that Edward had fashioned to get into this room, and felt around for something, anything that would give a hint as to how to open it. He was clever like Brandan, he could do anything.

I pressed against the lower left front corner and as if by magic, it lifted swiftly and silently. A false bottom! Inside was filled with rocks—hundreds of rocks. Gold—nuggets, some looking like rocks, some like pure gold. I needed to get to Brandan. Leaving everything exactly as I found it, I dressed quickly. It was four o'clock in the morning, but I needed to tell him.

Clearly speeding through the Canyon, I was to the hospital within half an hour. When I arrived they told me nothing had changed, but I wanted to be with him. I felt a sense of desperation when I saw him in the same position. "Brandan," I whispered. "Brandan, I need you. You need to wake up soon, it's not okay for you to continue to sleep like this. I'm not going to let you leave me, do you understand?" I spoke quietly to him for as long as they allowed me to stay.

I continued to give him words of encouragement throughout the day. Careful to avoid the monitor wires and IVs, I climbed into bed with him when we were alone. "Listen, I love you. I don't want to be here anymore. I want to be in our bed in our house lying next to each other with twinkling lights around us, talking about things we want to do and babies we want to have together. Okay? So here's my case. You wake up and come home and I'll marry you. How's that sound?

"The way I look at it, the house belongs to you more than me. Good grief, has it registered that *you* are the direct descendant of Edward and Jordan? The house is more yours than mine. So I'll split it with you as a wedding gift. And I'll give you the trunk in the closet, and you don't even know what that means yet, but I'm desperate here. Deal? Please, Brandan, don't let Simon win again."

Nothing changed from visit to visit. "Brandan, you have to wake up now. I found the mother lode, and you're the only one I can tell about it. Please, what good does any of this do if you're not here to share it with me?" My tears wet his cheek, I tenderly wiped them away. "I'm not going anywhere, do you understand? You can't get out of your promise to marry me just because you got shot. I won't lose that easily."

Miles and I spoke on the phone throughout the day. He was involved with something, but told me he'd get to the hospital soon. Brandan had been here several days when Miles showed up—with Jeni! "Oh, my God! When did you get here?!" I was thrilled to see her.

"Miles picked me up from the airport. We drove straight here. He thought you might need me."

"Oh, Miles, thank you. I love you," I said, holding on to Jeni like a lifeline. "Oh, honey, you could ill afford the time away, but I'm not going to complain. I'm so thankful you're here."

We sat in the waiting room talking for almost an hour. When I looked at my watch, I jumped up and said, "I'll be back soon. I get to visit him again for a while."

"I'll wait for you right here," Jeni said, touching my face. "It's gonna be all right, sweetheart."

"Keep telling me that. I need to believe it."

The nurse was kind enough to leave us alone when I entered. I went to the bed and ran my fingers through his hair as I had done so many times, kissing him, telling him how much he meant to me, how he had to wake up now. I told him I'd made the best discovery of all, but he needed to be looking me in the eye before I could tell him. I told him I would marry him the minute he woke up, but he had to wake up for that to happen. And I told him how much I loved him. I spent a half an hour with him, pouring out my heart, believing it was all going to work out. I couldn't survive the alternative.

Jeni and I went to lunch. Miles was missing when we came back so I texted him. He immediately responded with, "I'm with Brandan. Come back."

The look on Miles' face was devastating. He shook his head and turned to what appeared to be the hospital chaplain. "NO!" I shouted. "What's *he* doing here? NO!" I said again.

"I'm sorry, Jordan," Miles said, hugging me as he left the room.

"What?!" I asked, looking toward the chaplain, looking toward the nurse. "*Tell me!*"

"Stop shouting like that or they'll make you leave. Are you trying to wake the dead?" Brandan asked quietly from the bed, slowly opening his eyes.

"Brandan!" I ran to him, hugging him, sobbing. "You're awake!"

"Yeah, have been for a little while."

"What do you mean?" I asked, looking from the nurse to the chaplain and back to Brandan. "How *long* have you been awake?"

"Long enough to hear you say you'd marry me the minute I woke up. You're not backing out on that promise, are you?" he asked weakly.

"Why didn't you say something?"

"I was enjoying hearing all the things you wouldn't have said if I'd been awake. It will probably be the only time in our relationship I'll have to fake it," he said with a wicked grin that turned to a grimace of pain.

The door opened. Jeni and Miles stepped in. Jeni was grinning like a Cheshire Cat and gave me a thumbs up. "What's going on?"

The nurse stepped forward, checking Brandan's vital signs. "Ma'am, you're not allowed to visit like this if you're not family. Mr. Webb is willing to overlook that violation if you would like to become family," she said with a smile on her face.

"Now?" I asked, incredulous.

"His vitals are good. He's turned a corner. We're going to be releasing him to a regular room shortly. Chaplain Hammond is ready to make it legal."

I walked over to the bed and bent close. "Are you sure?" I asked, looking him in the eye.

"Never more sure of anything in my life," he said in a weak, raspy voice.

"But I have to tell you something. I have to tell you in private."

"Jordan, I don't care if you've found a pot of gold at the end of the rainbow. There's nothing you can say or do that's gonna change my mind."

Jeni stepped forward and handed me a flower. Miles took her hand. Two nurses stood to the side of the bed and raised the head of his bed. Brandan looked alert, the color returning to his cheeks. He nodded to the chaplain.

"Dearly beloved . . ."

THE END

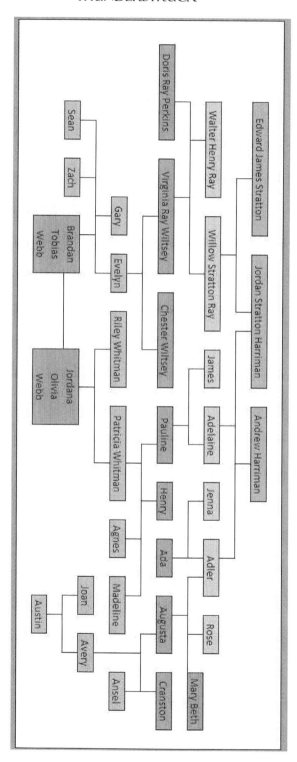

THUNDER STORM

BOOK THREE IN THE
THUNDER ON THE MOUNTAIN SERIES
SCHEDULED FOR RELEASE SPRING 2014

It wasn't fair that she should be the one being buried. Even the skies mourned, and wept with us. The drizzle turned to sleet as the black cars snaked their way through the streets of Brooklyn. The sun had not made an appearance in days, adding another layer to the dreamlike quality of the past week. It was all closing in, including the clouds that were now low enough to weave their tentacles around the slow-moving procession.

The reality of her death had not yet registered. "I'll come see you tonight, I promise," I had told her. "I'm sorry I haven't been there this week, but landing this new client has been a year in the making. It'll rocket my little company into the stratosphere. This is what I've been working so hard for, and trust me, it's a coup."

But I didn't make it that night. A last-minute call from the new client lasted almost two hours. When I phoned to tell her what happened, she didn't answer. I figured they were doing their nighttime routine. I tried several more times, and again the following morning, but my calls went unanswered. By noon I was concerned enough to take an extended lunch to check on them.

The front door was locked, and no one answered the bell. I used my key. "Mama? You here?" The dishes sat neatly in the strainer on the counter. "Mama?" I opened her bedroom door. They were both in her bed.

"*Mama!*" I cried, seeing her lifeless body in the arms of the woman who had given her birth.

"She's so cold," said my grandmother. "I thought I could warm her if I held her."

"Oh, Mama!" I sobbed, taking her in my arms.

"Hush, now. You're gonna wake her, and she's so tired. Hasn't moved all morning."

"Oh, Nana, come with me, darling, let's get you dressed." I wept as I tried to get her out of bed.

"Jeni's gonna be here soon. She'll know what to do."

I called the coroner's office. "Please send an ambulance."

"Who are you?" my grandmother asked.

"I'm here to help you. Let's get you dressed, sweetheart, before the men show up."

These had been the three saddest days of my existence. Shards of ice cut across the glassy rooftop of the limousine. I pressed my chest as we left the cemetery, trying to relieve the pain. I wouldn't have made it without Jordan. "What's the immediate plan? I'll stay for the week and will do as much as I can to make your life easier." She rubbed my fingers.

"I appreciate that, but what about Brandan? Won't he be upset with his bride being gone that long?"

"He gets stronger every day, and knows how important it is that you not be alone right now. Relax and let me be here for you like you always are for me. I'll get things as settled as possible before I head back," she said. She tucked another tissue into my hand.

"I haven't even faced her death yet. It was so unexpected, and I break down when I think of her."

"It'll take a while, Jeni. It's only been a few days."

"Here's what frightens me," I said, touching the necklace she had given me long ago. "Nana has dementia, the only person she knew is suddenly taken from her, and I just landed a national client that I've been wooing for over a year. I feel callous and selfish for trying to figure out how fast I can get back to work."

"Then we'll keep the nurse for another few days, and you'll go back to work tomorrow," she said in her take-charge, lawyer-like manner. "I'll interview the top five facilities that take patients with her issues, and I'll give you information to make an informed decision."

"There's no way . . ."

"There's no argument. It's done. If you think you can face it, you're going back tomorrow."

"What would I do without you, Jord? Do you know what an answer to prayer you are?"

"I'm in a state of shock myself. I can't imagine what you're going through."

Arriving back at the funeral home, the rain had slowed. Rays of sunshine peaked from behind bleak clouds. "That's the way it's going to be for you, darling. I promise, the sun will shine again soon."

The nursing home was one of the best for advanced care, and it was working out well. It was close enough that I could visit regularly, and the staff was considerate and experienced. As much as she was aware, Nana seemed to delight in being there. She had been there a few weeks when I got the call. "Ms. Jenkins?"

"Yes, this is Jeni."

"This is Leigh Ann from Fellowship Nursing Home. We're sorry to inform you that your grandmother walked out of an unlocked door this afternoon. We're doing everything we can to find her and will keep you updated."

If you enjoyed this book and would like to know of previous or future releases by Mimi Foster, please visit MimiFosterBooks.com. Leave your email address and we will contact you when other books are published.

STUFFED FRENCH TOAST

12 Pieces
Pepperidge Farm Cinnamon Bread OR
Pepperidge Farm Thin-sliced Bread OR
Bread of your choice – thinly sliced
1/2 block of Cream Cheese
2-3 tablespoons Strawberry Preserves OR
2-3 tablespoons Orange Marmalade OR jam of choice
EGG DIP
3-4 eggs
1 cup milk
1 tablespoon cinnamon
Splash of vanilla OR orange extract
Grease skillet. Pre-heat on medium-high temperature.

Mix cream cheese and marmalade (or jam); spread mixture on one slice of bread, then sandwich with another slice. Dip sandwich in egg mixture. Grill on greased skillet until both sides are browned. Cut in half diagonally and serve 3 halves per person, sprinkle with powder sugar. No syrup is necessary. Serves 4.

PUMPKIN PECAN PANCAKES WITH CIDER SYRUP

HOT CIDER SYRUP
¾ cup apple cider or juice
½ cup packed brown sugar
½ cup corn syrup
1 tablespoon butter
½ teaspoon lemon juice
Pinch of ground cinnamon
Pinch of ground nutmeg
PANCAKES
1 cup all-purpose flour
2 tablespoons sugar
2 teaspoons baking powder
½ teaspoon salt
½ teaspoon ground cinnamon
Pinch of nutmeg
Pinch of cloves
Pinch of ginger
Half to one cup chopped pecans
2 eggs, separated
1 cup milk
¾ cup canned pumpkin
2 tablespoons oil

1. In a large saucepan, combine syrup ingredients.
Bring to a boil over medium heat, stirring occasionally.
Reduce heat; simmer, uncovered, for 20-25 minutes or

until slightly thickened. Let stand for 30 minutes before serving.

2. For pancakes: In a large bowl, combine dry ingredients. In separate bowl, whisk egg *yolks*, milk, pumpkin, and oil until smooth. Stir in dry ingredients just until moistened. In a small bowl, beat egg *whites* until soft peaks form; fold into batter.

3. Pour batter by ¼ cupfuls onto a hot greased griddle. Turn when bubbles form on top of pancakes. Cook until second side is golden brown. Serve with syrup. Yield: 15 pancakes (1 cup syrup)

Made in the USA
Charleston, SC
07 January 2014